To Catch a Spy

An Ed Maddux novel

ALSO BY R.J. PATTERSON

Ed Maddux series
King of Queens
To Catch a Spy
Whispers of Treason

Cal Murphy series
Dead Shot
Dead Line
Better off Dead
Dead in the Water
Dead Man's Curve
Dead and Gone
Dead Wrong
Dead Man's Land
Dead Drop
Dead to Rights
Dead End

James Flynn series
The Warren Omissions
Imminent Threat
The Cooper Affair
Seeds of War

Brady Hawk series
First Strike
Deep Cover
Point of Impact
Full Blast
Target Zero
Fury
State of Play
Siege
Seek and Destroy
Into the Shadows

To Catch a Spy

an Ed Maddux novel

R.J. PATTERSON

FIRST EDITION

Cover art by Dan Pitts.

*For Jason Butler, a friend with a
passion for history and love for people*

There are some who become spies for money, or out of vanity and megalomania, or out of ambition, or out of a desire for thrills. But the malady of our time is of those who become spies out of idealism.

— MAX LERNER, *journalist*

I

OTTO VOSS AMBLED ALONG the sidewalk, casting glances over his shoulder to ensure no one followed him. Like most evenings after work, he kept his head down and his gait casual. Blending in was his goal. Yet after living in Prague for nearly twenty years, he remained puzzled as to why his acclimation to the Czech culture never seemed to arrive. A day rarely passed without him longing to return to his German homeland and the way things were before the war, but he knew such yearnings weren't likely to be fulfilled. He felt like a prisoner sentenced not to confinement in a cell but to eternal nomadic wandering. Such was the reality of a scientist working for the Nazis.

Voss checked once more behind him before hustling up the steps leading into his apartment. The elevator was in need of repair again, forcing him to make the hike up twelve flights of stairs to his suite located atop the building, not that he minded the extra time alone. He often wished there was more time to unwind from a stressful day working at the joint Russian-Czech propulsion lab.

After he strode through the door, Ingrid was there to greet him with a kiss.

Despite spending most of his time trying to forget what he'd lost, Ingrid appeared as an oasis in his desert of sorrow. Voss met her not long after he and more than a dozen other colleagues sought refuge in Prague from the vengeful U.S. forces. Her silky voice had a soothing effect on Voss, often the only thing that could settle his nerves when alcohol was in short supply. She told him she understood how he felt since she, too, once lived in Berlin. A year later, they married. Another eight years passed before she became pregnant and gave birth to Astrid.

"Papa, you're home!" Astrid said as she crashed into Voss's waist and wrapped her arms around him.

Voss stooped down and rubbed her on the head. "How was school today?"

"Great," she said. "I made a new friend."

"That's wonderful, dear. What's her name?"

"*His* name is Hans," she said.

"A boy? I didn't know you had friends who were boys."

"I don't. Just him. But it's only because of his middle name."

"And what's that?"

"Otto—just like you, Papa."

"Well, I imagine he must be a fine young man then."

"He is. He stood up for me when I-when I . . ."

Voss looked deep into his daughter's eyes. "Go on, you can say it."

"When I started to st-st-stutter."

Voss hugged Astrid. "Sounds like you're a good judge of character."

"I love you, Papa," she said before skipping off to her room.

He waited until he heard Astrid's bedroom door shut before he spoke.

"Children can be such monsters," Voss said to Ingrid.

She nodded as she grabbed his hand and led him to the kitchen. "Children or children in Prague?" she asked. "Because there are ways to address such issues."

Voss rounded the corner and looked up to see a familiar man standing next to the stove.

"Gregory Mikhailov," Voss said with a sigh. "You are one relentless man."

Mikhailov, dressed in a suit and smoking a cigarette, extended his hand to Voss, which he ignored. "Perhaps *stubborn* is a better description, a description that also applies to you."

"And when an irresistible force and an immovable object meet, do you know what happens?"

"I'm not the physicist," Mikhailov said. "Why don't you tell me?"

"My question is not one for science. It is a philosophical one and is more commonly known as the irresistible force paradox."

Mikhailov took a long drag and exhaled a plume of smoke. "I'm not a philosopher either."

"Well, I guess we're about to find out the answer together," Voss said, "because I have no intention of enlisting in your idiotic mission."

Mikhailov shot a quick glance at Ingrid before directing his focus back to Voss. "Have you forgotten what the allies did to us during the war?"

Voss shook his head. "The allies did nothing to you. In fact, you fought with them. You Russians need to brush up on your history."

"No, perhaps you are the one who needs a history lesson, for you see Russia was forgotten in all of the rebuilding efforts. We were the international dumping grounds, both for bodies and for rubble. The allies seemed intent on rebuilding Europe, but they left my country out of it. They used us to win their war, a war that we paid a higher price for than any other country. And while the United States and her allies go on to enjoy such wealth and privilege, mother Russia is left to care for her fatherless children while living in squalor."

"Spare me your history lesson," Voss said, waving dismissively at Mikhailov. "Do you know what would happen if they caught me? I worked for the Nazis. I did monstrous things in the name of science, things I don't care to ever think about again. But they don't care about that. If they look me up and discover I worked with Johannes Stark, they will make a public spectacle of me and my family. My life in Prague is less than desirable, but it is far better than a humiliating death."

Ingrid eased next to her husband and gently rubbed his back.

"Don't be so hasty in your decision, dear," she said. "There might be a way we can all get what we want here. You and I want a fresh start and a good place for Astrid to grow up. Mr. Mikhailov wants information that could protect people on this side of the world. We don't have to be adversaries anymore."

Voss twisted away from Ingrid. "Mr. Mikhailov doesn't want to protect anyone. He wants to start another war."

Mikhailov blew another stream of smoke into the air. "I'll give you until tonight to think about it."

"I've already made my decision," Voss said. "And for the third time, it is still no."

"I'm disappointed in you, Otto," Mikhailov said. "I thought you had changed."

Voss nodded toward the door. "You can show yourself out."

Mikhailov lumbered to the exit before stopping and turning back to look at Voss.

"You're going to change your mind one day, Otto," Mikhailov said, pointing at Voss with the pair of fingers clutching the cigarette.

"Never. Now, don't let me ever see you in my apartment again."

"You have a beautiful daughter and a lovely family, but what if something happened to them?"

"Get out now," Voss yelled.

"It'd be a terrible thing if something did." Mikhailov exited the apartment, leaving the door open, which Voss stormed across the room to slam shut.

Ingrid leaned against the doorjamb leading to the kitchen.

"We need to think about what he said, dear," she said.

Voss narrowed his eyes. "We don't need to think about anything. Did you hear what he *just* said? He threatened you. He threatened Astrid."

"I'm sure he was just trying to scare you."

"Well it worked. Besides, it's your fault that this keeps happening. Why did you let him in our home in the first place? I told you before that I never wanted to see that man again. All he does is make trouble for us—and now he's crossed the line. We're not going to be spies in the United States for him. Not now, not ever."

"But what about Astrid?" she asked. "It would do her good to be in an environment that wasn't so harsh as what we have here in Prague. She gets made fun of every day. What would've happened to her if Hans hadn't come to her rescue today?"

"There will always be a bully and there will be a Hans," he said. "Do you not think America has bullies?"

"No, but I think they have more children like Hans."

Voss laughed heartily. "Oh, Ingrid, you are more naïve than you look. And that is not an easy task to accomplish."

"Do not mock me," she said. "I only want what is best for our daughter. I'm sorry that you don't feel the same way."

"My decision to reject Mikhailov's offer is not directly related to how I feel about our daughter. I absolutely want the best for her, but I know the best does not require me to put all of us at risk, never mind the fact that it's entirely possible she could witness her father being ridiculed and harassed and possibly even killed for my own past indiscretions. Could you possibly think that's what would be best for our daughter?"

A loud creak in the hallway put a halt to the conversation.

Voss turned his gaze away from Ingrid only to see Astrid standing a few feet away and clutching her doll.

"Why are you two fighting?" Astrid asked. "I don't like it when you shout, Papa."

Voss moved toward Astrid, but she withdrew, turning quickly and running toward her room.

He looked back at his wife, only to catch her glaring at him.

"Don't blame me," he said. "I wasn't the one who allowed that agitator into our home."

Voss walked across the room and poured himself a glass of vodka. He settled down into his favorite chair and began reading the *Lidové Noviny,* Prague's most popular newspaper. He tried to forget about his tumultuous day and the events that ensued since he arrived home, a task that wasn't so easy due to the constant rattling of pots and pans from Ingrid while she finished preparing dinner.

* * *

AFTER A QUIET DINNER, Voss searched the house for his cigarettes. Unable to locate any, he announced to Ingrid that he was going to the store and would be back in a few minutes. He put on his hat and exited the apartment.

The rhythm of his steady gait down the steps was the only place Voss felt he could find solace, given how his day had gone. At work, the pressure to develop more accuracy for lunar rockets had reached a fever pitch. On his way home, Voss felt the ever-present eyes of the StB, the Czechoslovakian secret police, lurking on every corner. Then there was Ingrid's contentious demeanor, the result of a wife living more or less a caged life in a foreign country. She'd grown increasingly antsy over the past few months, and Voss could almost feel a palpable tension. But amidst the echoing chamber of stairs, those problems vanished. His could clear his head, even if just for a moment, without fear of being followed or accosted. Twelve flights of stairs had become too short for Voss's taste and lacked the time necessary to appropriately mull over an escape plan.

Though he was barely twenty-five years old when the war ended, his exposure to allied troops and their Marlboro cigarettes was enough to create an addiction. Voss tried not to smoke that often, but whenever he became stressed, he craved them. The crackle of the tobacco when it first caught fire, the sudden relief he experienced the moment he filled his lungs with smoke—it was a vice that maintained a grip on him whether he was stressed or not, if he was to be honest. But the allure seemed particularly strong on days like the one he was having.

Once Voss arrived at the store on the corner, he purchased a pack of Marlboros and wasted little time in lighting up. He was in the middle of a long drag when a bald, stumpy man interrupted Voss's moment of Zen.

"Those things will kill you," the man said, hitting Voss on the arm.

Voss removed the cigarette before exhaling. He held it arm's length and studied it for a moment. "I doubt this little thing will be what does me in."

The man smiled and shook Voss's hand.

"Fedor Babinski," Voss said. "What are you doing here? I thought you were in prison."

"Smuggling restricted items into the country is frowned upon, but not eternally, especially when you can supply the judge with his favorite bourbon from America."

"So, what are you doing now?" Voss asked.

"Something much more noble."

"Oh? Such as?"

"Have you plotted out the end of your life?" Babinski asked.

"Someone's already plotting the ending for me—and I imagine it will come sooner than later."

Babinski glanced around before leaning in close to Voss, who'd settled comfortably against the outside wall of the store.

"What if I told you that you could write your own ticket out of here? Maybe get away to a place where your every movement down the street isn't being watched?"

"Does this place also happen to be lacking Nazi hunters?"

Babinski chuckled. "If you're looking to get away from them, good luck. They're everywhere these days. But I think I can get you to a place where no one will ask questions or even consider the possibility you were once a Nazi scientist."

Voss glared at the man. "I was a never a Nazi—I just worked for them. I had no choice."

"Of course you didn't. None of us did during those times, but we did it anyway."

"Willingly or coerced—it doesn't seem to matter to anyone much these days."

"Well, you don't have to stay here forever, or even another night."

Voss took another drag and stared out at the street in front of him. "What are you suggesting, Babinski? Do you have a plan?"

Babinski smiled and rubbed his head. "Not only do I have a plan, but I have a car waiting for you and your family. Meet me in the alley behind your apartment in one hour, and I will personally transport you across the border to a safe place where you will be able to receive political asylum."

"That is quite the proposition. How do I know you're telling me the truth?"

"I have access to a private plane and airstrip in the Sudetes. Once I get you across the border, I'll take you to a German outpost. They will grant your asylum and present you with legal travel papers."

"And after that?"

"I will take you to any free country you wish, though I would like to recommend somewhere in South America as a final destination."

"South America?"

Babinski nodded. "Yes, the Europeans don't go poking their noses down there very often. You can live in a secure enclave in a nice part of Rio or Buenos Aires. It's all about whether you want to learn Portuguese or Spanish."

"And how will I live?"

"As a free man."

Voss scowled. "I'm talking about my money. How will I get it there?"

"There is a price for freedom, Mr. Voss. And I believe you'll find it far exceeds anything you have in your bank account. But I can make arrangements to wire your money to you once your family arrives, minus our fees of course. It's all part of our services."

Voss took a deep breath and then exhaled slowly.

"One hour," Voss said, glancing at his watch. "I'll meet you in the alley in one hour."

Babinski flashed a grin. "Excellent decision, Mr. Voss, because I wasn't going to offer it to you again."

Voss maintained his normal casual pace as he returned home. However, once he was inside, he resembled more of a whirling dervish. Rushing about the house, he stuffed his most prized possessions into a suitcase and urged Ingrid and Astrid to do the same.

"Otto, Otto," Ingrid said. "What are you doing?"

"Papa, is everything okay?" Astrid asked.

Voss paused and looked intently at the two women in his life. A faint smile spread across his lips as he nodded. "Yes, everything is more than okay," he said. "Everything is amazing."

Astrid joined him in his delight, her eyes twinkling as she looked at her father. Ingrid, however, didn't share the same feelings.

"You still haven't answered my question, Otto. What are you doing?"

He firmly grabbed his wife's shoulders and stared into her eyes. "We're getting out of here right now. In less than one hour, a man will meet us downstairs and transport us to freedom. Do you understand what this means?"

Ingrid nodded imperceptibly.

"No, I don't think you do," Voss said. "It means we can be free."

"Free? Do you even know what you're saying? You think they're just going to let you walk away after what you know?"

"No, but it means I will get to die on my own terms. That is all the freedom I have right now, and it's far better than raising our daughter in a caged world."

Ingrid cocked her head to one side, lines rippling across her forehead. "I don't know, Otto. It sounds so risky. Who is this man? How do you know you can even trust this man?"

"Fedor Babinski."

"That crook? How can you trust *him*?"

"I can't, but he's a smuggler, so he's done this before."

"Smuggling liquor isn't the same as smuggling people."

"You're probably right, but Mikhailov left us with no choice after his threat earlier today."

"I don't like it, Otto."

"I don't care if you don't like it. If we're going to escape, we're going to have to trust someone. And to be fair, I can hardly trust anyone these days, including you."

"Otto! How dare you say such a thing? You know I will stand with you anywhere."

"I'd always hoped as much, but I guess we're going to find out if that's true or not because I'm leaving in less than an hour with Astrid. The choices are simple: take our chances with Mikhailov and remain in our miserable lives here, or seize a chance at freedom right now. The choice left for you is whether or not you care to join us."

"I wouldn't want to be anywhere else, but—"

"There is no time to place qualifiers on our decisions or our beliefs. We must simply act and hope for the best. Now go grab your things, for we will never see this place again after tonight."

Ingrid nodded and scurried to the closet in search of her luggage.

At the appointed time, Voss led his family down the back stairwell and into the alleyway. And waiting for them was Babinski, just as he had promised.

"The ride won't be comfortable," Babinski said as he opened the trunk and gestured for them to get inside. "But it will be a long lost memory once you attain your freedom."

One by one, the Voss family piled into the trunk—Otto first, followed by Ingrid, then Astrid.

"Is everyone comfortable?" Voss asked.

"As comfortable as we can be," Ingrid said.

"Astrid?"

"Yes, Papa."

"Are you frightened?"

"No, Papa. I'm with you and Mama. What do I have to fear?"

Voss groped in the darkness for her head and rubbed it.

"You're right, my dear. There is nothing to fear. In a few short hours, we will all be free."

The engine sputtered and coughed to life before Mr. Babinski stepped on the accelerator and the car lurched forward.

"I already feel like the burden is lifting," Voss said, pulling Ingrid and Astrid tight. "It won't be long now."

II

ED MADDUX PEERED THROUGH a pair of binoculars at the warehouse near the bottom of the hill and made mental notes of the scenario. His mission was relatively simple in nature: recapture a prisoner who'd been made as a spy by a Russian contingent. According to all the intelligence reports that Maddux had, the KGB wasted little time with low-level CIA assets. The less a person knew, the less valuable—and the more easily discarded. Arthur Butler fit that profile and wouldn't have more than thirty-six hours to live after he'd been taken before the Russian contingent learned his true value, and thirty-five hours had passed. The pressure of rescuing Butler in less than an hour weighed heavily on Maddux.

Creeping down the mountainside, Maddux used his long-range rifle to tranquilize a pair of guards, clearing a three-minute window to scramble down to the building where Butler was being held, free him, and escape back into the woods. Executing the plan flawlessly, Maddux untied Butler, who headed directly for the thick forest. Maddux glanced at his watch. He had thirty seconds to clear the premises and get a head start on the Russians before they discovered the downed guards. But something went wrong.

Upon exiting the shed where Butler had been held, Maddux noticed a flurry of activity out of the corner of his eye. However, what he saw in front of him provided the most cause for concern: an armed guard returning from the woods to relieve himself, head down.

Change of plans.

Maddux doubled back in order to use the building for cover. He figured he'd have just enough time to escape the guard and vanish into the woods. But it was a poor miscalculation.

Rounding the corner, Maddux caught a glimpse of the soldier, who was right on Maddux's six. He decided to make a dash for the woods any way. He'd already secured the asset and figured he could outrun the man in pursuit. Maddux's misstep cost him dearly.

A searing pain ripped through Maddux's back, forcing him immediately to his knees. He stumbled for a few steps before crashing to the earth with a thud. His back felt like it was on fire, while his vision blurred. A few seconds later, Maddux was unconscious.

* * *

MADDUX AWOKE TO FIND himself strapped to a table inside a sterile building. A doctor hovered over him, poking and prodding his extremities before shining a light in his eyes.

"I think he looks fine," the doctor said. "He's all yours."

Maddux squinted, trying to make out the man striding toward the bed. As his face came into view, Maddux sighed.

"You're not exactly the person I wanted to see right now," Maddux said.

Charles Pritchett chuckled as he used his hook and his left hand to unstrap Maddux.

"Your training, whether you like it or not, consists of great ups and downs. And while you've mostly been up, this exercise was the exact opposite. It's a good lesson in how to get killed."

"You don't think I know that already?" Maddux said as the bindings released, enabling him to sit up.

"Since everything here is about becoming a skilled field agent, tell me, what could you have done differently?"

"Probably waited in the building a little longer to make sure the grounds were clear of any guards."

Pritchett shrugged. "Maybe that would've mattered. Maybe it wouldn't have. You couldn't have known that there would be a guard returning from the bathroom, despite all the intel you were given about the movements of the security personnel in and around the facility. And while it was a wrinkle we added to see how you'd adapt in a live simulation, you will deal with flies in the ointment all the time. How you handle them is what will make you a good agent."

"So, what else could I have done?" Maddux asked.

"Exactly what you did do, except for the dash toward the woods. That was your fatal mistake, for it would've been a bullet, not a tranquilizer dart that would've pierced your back."

"If I come out in the open and see the guard, are you suggesting that I turn and shoot him, drawing more attention to myself?"

Pritchett shook his head. "Absolutely not. You would've circled the building and taken up a position on the back. When the guard rounded the corner, you would've blindsided him before incapacitating him in some manner."

"And what if someone saw me?"

Pritchett smiled. "That would've been my favorite part. I would've aimed for the large gas tank on the other side of the property to create a diversion. Putting out that fire would've suddenly become their top priority, and they would've shrugged about a low-level CIA asset and his rescuer getting away."

"You like explosions, don't you?"

"Not as much as you might think," Pritchett said as he pointed to the patch covering his right eye.

"Shrapnel?" Maddux asked.

"Something like that. But I don't have time to tell that story right now. What I do need to tell you is that I've got a meeting with the committee this evening to determine if you're field operational."

"If I'm not?"

"Several more weeks of training."

"And if I am?"

"You'll be heading to Bonn by the end of the week."

Maddux smiled. "What do you think? Am I ready?"

"That's going to be my recommendation, even today withstanding. You have good instincts, though sometimes—like today—survival requires that you ignore your mental reflexes and do something entirely different. I'm confident that you'll figure this out before you make a costly mistake. And we'll do our best to keep your first missions simple."

"I'd appreciate that," Maddux said. "I feel more and more confident each time out, but in every training exercise, I can't deny that I had a twinge of fear."

"Those twinges are what keep us alive, Ed. The truly fearless ones are the agents who end up dead in their prime. Fear isn't always a bad thing to have."

* * *

LATER THAT EVENING, Pritchett settled into a comfortable chair across the table from CIA operations director Harold Tillman at the Occidental Grill in Washington, D.C. Pritchett had made the two-hour drive down from the CIA's secret training facility nestled in the Shenandoah Mountains. He ordered a drink and watched Tillman slowly flip through page after page of Pritchett's report on the most recent class of civilian recruits assigned to overseas posts.

"Looks like we have an impressive bunch of men and women," Tillman finally said after shutting the file folder.

"Most impressive, indeed."

Tillman clasped his hands and leaned forward on the table.

"Most of the students spent nine months to a year there, but Mr. Ed Maddux only spent about six months there," Tillman said. "How does he compare to the rest of the class?"

"He's on par with them, if not a step ahead."

Tillman pulled his glasses out and opened the folder before pointing to Maddux's name.

"But it says on the report he failed his final mission."

"We had a chat about that."

Tillman looked over the top of his glasses. "A chat?

You think that's all it takes to correct a terribly misguided decision in the field."

"To be fair, I did increase the level of difficulty quite significantly."

"And how do our top agents fair under similarly controlled circumstances?"

Maddux shook his head. "About half pass."

Tillman looked pensively at the report on Maddux.

"Even still, I'm not sure he's ready. You want to assign him to Bonn. Do you know the level of expertise to navigate Germany and the rest of Eastern Europe? One slip up like this and the chat you'll be having is with his next of kin."

"If only."

Tillman scowled. "What's that supposed to mean?"

"Forget it. I just think he's ready or else I wouldn't have presented this to you. At some point you've got to push the bird out of the nest to see if it will fly."

"But this bird is so strategically placed that I'd hate to see him fall to earth—and be buried under it—on his first flight."

"Look, I oversaw some of his training personally, and I'll be moving on to serve as station chief in Bonn next week. I can assure you that he will be teamed with a competent agent and given missions that will not exceed his skill level."

Tillman took a long pull on his glass of bourbon before setting it down hard on the table. "Okay," he said. "I'll relent. If you feel he's ready and you can assure me that he won't be compromised in any way during these early missions, I'll release him."

"Excellent," Pritchett said. "I think this class is going

to impress you."

"You better be right."

* * *

MADDUX HAD SETTLED INTO BED with a book when someone rapped on the door of his dorm-style room at the training facility. Throwing on some clothes, Maddux strode to the door and answered it.

"There's a call for you, Mr. Maddux," the man said, pointing toward the bank of phones at the end of the hall.

Maddux shuffled along the floor until he reached the dangling receiver. He picked it up and answered. "This is Ed Maddux."

"Maddux, Pritchett here. You're in. Tillman approved you, and you'll need to ship out in the morning at 9:00 a.m. Have all your personal effects ready to go by then."

"I haven't even packed up my house."

"We'll have someone do that for you."

"Thank you, Pritchett. I won't let you down."

"You better now. It's my head on the chopping block if you do."

Maddux hung up and glided back to his room. He started to pack up his belongings, entertained by passing thoughts regarding his father as well as what his future life in Germany would be like. While his inclination was to romanticize his life as a spy, he knew better. His existence would likely be challenging, if not difficult. But he figured if it was half as rewarding as foiling the Russian plot to kill hundreds of people at the World's Fair, it'd be worth any amount of suffering.

He was about halfway done packing when he

realized he'd checked in a few personal items at the front desk. As he was on his way to retrieve them, one of the instructors stopped him.

"Maddux, right?" the teacher said, pointing.

Maddux nodded.

"I know I didn't have any classes with you, but I just want to say you look so familiar. You're not related to a John Hambrick, are you?"

Maddux shook his head. "Never heard of the guy. Should I have?"

The instructor shrugged. "I don't know, but you look just like him."

"He worked for the agency?"

The man nodded. "I saw him maybe ten or twelve years ago. I'd swear you two were related. You're a spitting image of him."

"Where'd you meet him?"

"One of my tours oversees? I can't remember exactly where though—maybe Italy, maybe France or Germany. I'm too old to recall all those little details any more."

"Well, thanks for letting me know," Maddux said. "Maybe if I run into a John Hambrick one day, I'll ask him."

"Oh, I don't think he's with the agency any more. In fact, I'd be surprised if he was. He'd either have a cushy desk job by now or he'd be retired."

John Hambrick? Good to know.

Maddux's thoughts shifted to being consumed with those of his father. Maddux figured if he stuck around long enough, he'd be able to piece something together and find his old man, one way or another.

III

NEAR THE CZECHOSLOVAKIA BORDER

TWO HOURS INTO THEIR RIDE, Otto Voss let out a long sigh of relief when Mr. Babinski's car lurched to a halt. Voss knew they weren't over the border since they never stopped and weren't checked, but he knew they weren't far. Voss squeezed Ingrid and Astrid again, assuring them with a gentle whisper that it would all be over soon.

A car door slammed followed by the sound of feet crunching slowly away in a gravel parking lot. A couple minutes later, the sound of footsteps drawing nearer ended abruptly when Voss heard a key inserted into the trunk. It creaked as it opened, and Babinski lifted the secret compartment and cast a shadow over his three stowaways. He handed them a cup of water.

"Share it quickly," he said. "I need to keep moving. We'll be at the gate in less than half an hour."

He didn't wait long before shutting the trunk.

Time passed slowly as they pulled back onto the road and rumbled along toward the German border. Voss had nothing to do but think. Doubt and fear crept into his mind, causing him to second guess his decision.

What if I'd gone along with Mikhailov? I could've made a break for it in the U.S. or maybe even become a double agent. That would've been smarter than this. What was I thinking?

Sweat beaded on his forehead with an occasional drip downward onto Ingrid. He knew she could feel it, but she remained silent. The farther they drove, the more regret Voss had.

Finally, the car rolled to a stop, the brakes squealing loudly. The engine idled and Voss listened as a Czech officer and Babinski engaged in a brief conversation. The inspection was minimal, which surprised Voss. He listened intently and thought he heard what sounded like one guard circling the car with a dog. No one even opened the trunk, though they were tucked into a hidden compartment and covered with a dark blanket in the off chance that a clever officer managed to find it.

The guard tapped the side of the car, and it started to move again.

After a minute, Ingrid finally spoke in a whisper. "Did we make it?"

"I hope so," Voss said. "We still have to cross the German border."

They came to another stop and the same process repeated itself, only this time the guards spoke German instead of Czech.

Returning to the road, the car bumped along for another couple minutes before stopping again. This time, the engine was turned off. Babinski opened the truck and then the compartment.

"You're here," he said with a big grin on his face.

He reached in to help Astrid out first, followed by Ingrid then Voss.

A guard wearing a U.S. insignia on the sleeve of his uniform nodded at Babinski.

"So, what do you have for us tonight, Mr. Babinski?" the soldier asked.

Voss dropped his shoulders and exhaled. *They know each other. What was I ever worried about?*

The guard turned to Voss. "Papers, please."

Voss fumbled around in his pocket for a moment before retrieving the passports Babinski had given him. They contained names of different identities, anything to protect the Americans from learning about Voss's past.

"Wait here one moment while I check with my commander about this," the guard said before disappearing.

"Do you think something is wrong?" Ingrid asked with an edge to her voice.

Babinski shook his head and waved dismissively. "It's standard protocol. You will be fine. Trust me."

After five minutes, the guard returned.

"Thank you, Mr. Babinski. You can leave their possessions right here, and we'll take them from here."

Babinski spun toward the car and retrieved the Voss family luggage. He set it on the ground and shook Voss's hand.

"What about your private plane to take us anywhere we wish?" Voss asked.

"Tomorrow," Babinski said. "You'll stay here overnight while they make sure that you're no threat, which of course we know you aren't. I'll just be down the road at a nearby hostel. No need to worry."

Another guard hustled out and snagged the suitcases, toting them inside.

"What are they doing?" Ingrid asked.

"They're just inspecting your things," the head guard said.

"What for?"

"You've been living in a country run by deceitful and powerful forces. You never know what might end up being sewn into your waistband or tucked beneath the sole of your shoe. The Russians are masters at hiding listening devices. It's embarrassing how many times we've been tricked."

Voss nodded. "We understand."

"Good," the guard said, offering his hand. "I'm Lieutenant Gerald Franklin, the commander of this outpost."

Voss shook his hand. "William Richards. And this is my wife Ingrid and my daughter Astrid."

Babinski had instructed Voss to keep his wife and daughter's first names the same to avoid any potential slip up. But they all had the last name Richards on their fake passport, a point Voss emphasized to Astrid during their ride so she wouldn't blow the family's cover.

"Let's step inside, shall we?" Franklin said.

Voss led his family into the wooden slat board building. It appeared to contain four enclosed offices and a small open area for visitors. They all took a seat once they entered the outpost, Franklin positioned directly across from Voss.

"So, Mr. Richards, tell me about your background. What is it that you do for a living?"

"I sell tires, mostly to the Czech and Russian governments," Voss said.

"And this has created an issue that requires you to have political asylum?"

Voss nodded. "It has. I've been threatened for holding views that are essentially neutral when it comes to the allies versus Russia and the Eastern Bloc. I simply want freedom."

Franklin chuckled. "Well, that's something that's in short supply where you just came from, that's for sure."

He glanced over at a couple of bottles of Kentucky bourbon sitting in the corner of the room and then back at Voss.

"Would you like some of that? Good ole fashioned bourbon from the United States."

"What exactly does it taste like?" Voss asked.

"It tastes like freedom," Franklin said with a hearty laugh before standing up and striding across the room.

He poured a couple of glasses and walked toward his seat.

"Here, Mr. Richards, why don't you try it yourself?"

Voss accepted the glass, quickly gulping down the drink. He wiped his mouth with the back of his hand and set the cup down on the floor beneath his chair.

"That is some stout drink," Voss said.

"Aha! So you like it?" Franklin asked.

"Very much so."

"Good," Franklin said. "I can tell you're going to enjoy your newfound freedom in America."

Voss grinned as he watched another guard approach Franklin and whisper something in his ear. A furrowed brow replaced any hint of pleasure on Voss's face. Voss waited until the other guard left before speaking.

"Is there a problem?" Voss asked.

"I'm afraid I need to speak with you in private, Mr. Richards," Franklin said as he stood. He gestured toward the sole office that had an open door.

Voss stood slowly.

"What's wrong?" Ingrid asked.

"Nothing to worry about at this point," Franklin said. "Just protocol. We must speak to couples separate from one another to make sure stories align."

Voss narrowed his eyes as he looked at Franklin.

"Come, come," Franklin said, gesturing toward the door again. "I'm sure you'd all like to get a good night of sleep after riding in a cramped space for hours on end."

Voss walked cautiously toward the door. He felt dizzy and faint before a pounding headache stormed on.

Franklin took a seat behind a desk, while one of the other guards shut the door behind him and remained in the room.

"Are you all right, Mr. Richards? Or should I say, Mr. Voss?"

Through blurring vision, Voss strained to see Franklin.

"What did you say?" Voss said, still trying to gather his wits.

"I think you heard me loud and clear, Mr. Voss."

Voss's body went limp as he crashed to the floor and then blacked out.

* * *

WHEN VOSS REGAINED consciousness, he was tied to a chair in a small room that was lit with a single overhead light. The bulb swayed back and forth in a rhythmic motion for quite a while, causing Voss to wonder how it maintained such steady movement. But that quickly ended when he tried to move his arms and felt the coarse rope digging into and burning his wrists.

The door opened and light flooded in from the outside. The silhouetted man quickly shut the door behind him and marched up to Voss.

"What's going on here?" Voss said. "What happened?"

"Apparently, you tried to sneak out of the Czech Republic, the one country that accepted Nazi scum without consequences, and into German territory controlled by the U.S., a country that doesn't care for Nazi scientists, such as yourself. Apparently, you were found out and they didn't want to waste time killing you, so they dumped you back off at the border and notified the guards that you were attempting to defect. And here you are."

"Just kill me, and get it over with," Voss said. "Just leave my family out of this. They had nothing to do with this. It was all my idea. I dragged them along."

The soldier shrugged. "If it were my place to help them, I would. But I'm afraid those kinds of decisions are over my head. However, I have one simple task, which would be made easier if you agree to comply with me."

"I'm not telling you anything if you can't guarantee my family's safety."

"For a man who swears his family had nothing to do with this, you sure seem determined to protect us from questioning them. That makes me want to *interrogate* them all the more, especially that pretty wife of yours, who's having the time of her life in the room next door."

The moment the guard stopped talking long enough to hear the heavy tension residing over the room, a blood-curdling scream came from down the hallway.

Ingrid.

"What are you doing to her?" Voss demanded.

"Nothing she doesn't deserve, that I can assure you."

"You better not hurt her because I swear if you do—"

The guard put his hand up, halting Voss. "Let me spare you the promises you will undoubtedly break. You will not do anything to me or anyone I know. But you will tell me what I want to know or suffer an excruciating death at my hands right here and now." He cracked his knuckles and stretched his arms. "Now, where to begin."

The guard circled Voss for a few moments.

"Do you have a name?" Voss asked, a desperate attempt to maintain a human connection with his captor.

"If it's all the same to you, I'd rather remain anonymous. It makes things much neater that way. Besides, I hate to hear people use my name as they hurl curses at me. It's so unbecoming." He continued circling Voss. "I guess we'll start with the chest," the guard said before unleashing a vicious punch into Voss's upper body.

Voss recoiled as much as he could and prepared for his thrashing. He endured several minutes of the guard's pounding—punches to the head, face, neck, arms, stomach, and groin area. A mixture of sweat and blood rolled down Voss's face and spilled into the corner of his eyes, making it difficult to see.

When the beating stopped, the real pain was the fact that he could hear Ingrid's screams next door. Then down the hall, an even fainter yet more haunting sound—that of Astrid calling for her parents.

"Papa! Mama!" she said. "I'm scared."

Her voice was enough to make Voss discover a

renewed sense of purpose. He couldn't die here. Not now, not like this.

"What *do* you want?" Voss finally asked, a question that managed to summon his abuser from the shadows.

The guard walked slowly back into the light as he wiped his hands clean of blood with a towel. "I thought you'd never ask."

* * *

SIX HOURS PASSED before Voss found himself standing outside the door of his Prague apartment, his clothes tattered and his face cut and bruised. The man who'd broken Voss promised that his family would be here when he arrived. And he was true to his word.

After Voss trudged up the twelve flights of steps, he didn't need to knock to enter his home. The door was halfway off the hinges. The entire apartment had been trashed and looted. What little furniture that remained had been reduced to splintered wood. Food had been spilled all over the kitchen floor. Beds had been removed.

Voss kicked himself for not being able to see it. Babinski had set him up somehow, and now Voss was assured a life of utter hell until he could legitimately escape the clutches of a government he once sought out as a safe haven.

He stepped over the debris cluttering the entryway and made his way toward Ingrid and Astrid. They were both sobbing.

"Why?" Ingrid asked, shoving away her husband. "Why did you do this to us?"

"I-I-I—"

He couldn't get the words out, not any that would

give his wife solace in the moment.

A feeble I'm sorry was all he could muster.

"Papa," Astrid said as she stood, "look."

She held up a handful of shredded paper. He could make out the faint colored images as pictures that his daughter once drew.

"They tore up my pictures," she said. "Why would they do that?"

He leaned down and got eye level with his daughter.

"There are some things in life that are too difficult to explain to you right now," he said. "But one day, I will tell you everything. I promise. Just know that your mama and I still love you no matter what happened or why these men did such mean things to us."

She reached out and touched a cut just below his eye.

"Do you need to go to the doctor?" she asked.

"I will be okay, dear."

He returned to his room and collapsed onto the floor. He fell asleep the moment his head hit the pillow, hoping to fall into a deep dream and never wake up.

* * *

A WEEK PASSED SLOWLY, and Voss's wounds started to heal on his face. But the anger and resentment remained. His time was filled with work during the day and repairs at night. By Friday evening, the apartment was returning to some semblance of order, though the furniture they got had to be either hand-me-downs or makeshift due to the fact that Voss's bank account had been drained.

Making the time move slowly was also the fact that Ingrid had yet to warm back up to her husband. If Voss managed to catch her looking at him, it was nothing more than a steely glare. She refused to sleep next to Voss, instead choosing to console Astrid, who woke up at least twice every night with nightmares.

Voss understood his daughter's fears. He had to admit that there was plenty to be afraid of. He had his own tormentors whenever the lights went out. The images of the Czech guard punishing him were ones he couldn't shake. He couldn't even dull his memories with vodka, his sustenance of choice since he'd returned home.

Voss was a quarter of a way through his Friday bottle when Mikhailov knocked on his door.

Voss opened the door, and his lifeless expression transformed into a cold glower almost instantaneously.

"You have a lot of nerve stopping by here," Voss said.

Mikhailov glanced down at Voss's bottle.

"Seems like you're handling things well."

"What do you want?"

"I wanted to see if you would reconsider my offer," Mikhailov said as he glanced around the apartment. "I'm willing to let the past stay in the past. Why don't we start over and forge an amicable relationship, maybe even a friendship?"

"If I didn't have so much vodka left in this bottle, I'd crack you over the head with it and then ram the jagged pieces into your throat."

Mikhailov widened his eyes. "I hope you don't think I did this. Because I would never do such a thing. Destroying a man's dignity is not how I operate."

"When did you turn over this new leaf?"

"Spare me your bitterness, Otto. You did this to

yourself. I offered you a way out, but you refused. Then you attempted to leave the country only to be rejected by those worthless Americans."

Voss took a long swig from the bottle.

"So now we're just going to march back across the border, and they're going to welcome me with open arms as if they don't know who I am."

"Well, you see, Otto, that was the problem all along. You pretended to be someone you weren't."

"And how do you know this?"

"William Richards—that was the name on the fake passports our soldiers at the border found on you. Perhaps you didn't know that William Richards is a Czech spy, something well known throughout the intelligence community at large. Now, had you attempted to cross into Germany using your given name, I think you would've made it."

"But I worked with the Nazis," Voss said. "You're forgetting that very important detail. I worked with Johannes Stark, no less. A monster in his own right."

"Perhaps, but I can supply you with a bit of worthless information to make them consider taking you in quite willingly," Mikhailov said. "Of course, we'd have to make the attempt at a different outpost, but what do you say? Willing to give it a try? Or would you like to sleep on the floor in this rat hole for the rest of your life? This is your final offer."

Voss turned over his shoulder and looked back into the kitchen at Ingrid, who nodded subtly. He understood her signal, knowing that she'd been listening in the entire time.

"We'll do it," Voss said.

"Excellent. I do apologize for your treatment last week. It was most unfortunate, but I'm sure you understand. We can't let people think they can attempt to defect and not have consequences."

"I just want revenge on the Americans for treating me like rubbish," Voss said.

Mikhailov smiled and shook his head.

"No, I'm sure the Americans aren't the only ones you'd like to get revenge against. But in case you have other ideas, just know that we can burn you any time we want. All it takes is one little call to the right people and you'll be facing a death sentence in land of so-called freedom."

"You won't have to worry about that."

"Good," Mikhailov said. "I didn't want to bring up such unpleasantries, but under the circumstances, I felt like it was necessary. Now, we'll be by tomorrow evening. So, gather all the things you'd like to take, though from the looks of your apartment, it appears there won't be much packing necessary. A car will be here at 6:00 p.m. sharp. I'll discuss the details and protocol for you to embed yourself among the American scientific community—and if we're lucky, with the U.S. Army's scientific brain trust."

"We'll be ready," Voss said as he shut the door.

He turned and looked at Ingrid, who wasn't scowling at him for the first time in a week.

"Are you sure you want to do this?" he asked.

She nodded. "See how easy this could've been had you gone along with his proposal the first time?"

Voss took another swig from his bottle.

"Now's not the time to dwell in the past, Ingrid. It's

over. We must look forward and hope that this next chapter of our lives isn't anywhere close to the hell that it has been recently."

She took the bottle out of his hand.

"What are you doing?" he asked.

"We have a long trip ahead of us tomorrow. It's time to get packing. And if you're going to be a spy, you're going to be a sober one."

MADDUX WAS STILL WAITING on his belongings
to arrive from New York when his new job sent him on
a short road trip from Bonn to the Frankfurt Motor
Show. While Maddux had been trained as a full-fledged
CIA operative, he remained classified as a civilian asset,
keeping his cover intact. The General Motors brass had
allowed for Maddux to take several months off under
the guise of a sabbatical before completing his transfer
from New York to the company's European car manufacturing arm, Opel. Maddux had split his training between physical instruction and German language class.
However, even the best sterile learning environment
couldn't have prepared Maddux for the cultural transi-
tion of living in Germany.

He quickly discovered that the good-natured ease
with which he handled his job in New York might as
well have been from another planet or another era alto-
gether. Casual and amicable interactions were the norm
among auto industry marketing executives in Maddux's
experience. Whether co-workers or rival companies,

conversations remained friendly and the industry looked out for its own as a whole. But not in Germany.

Stiff and stodgy characterized all business dealings, not to mention everyone seemed to play their cards close to the vest. Maddux would often hear at least one or two executives mention something about a new car in prototype that would trump the current hottest automobile on the market. But not in Frankfurt. Marketing directors from Mercedes-Benz and Volkswagen cast wary glances in his direction and whispered to their colleagues, likely about him.

Maddux attempted several conversations with others, but they ended abruptly. He didn't know if his unpolished accent gave him away, resulting in their disinterest. Or perhaps it was simply the fact that he was from Opel, a mid-level car competitor positioned perfectly between Mercedes's high-end automobiles and Volkswagen's more affordable ones. Maddux couldn't help but wonder if they all saw Opel as a threat to their business.

There's more than enough to go around. Stingy bastards.

Maddux ignored the chilly reception when the public address announcer reminded show attendees that Opel was about to reveal one of its prototypes destined for the production line in a few years. He smiled as one of the company's board members undraped the Opel GT. Maddux admitted it wasn't anywhere close to the Corvette or the Mustang, but for this niche of the European market, the car had potential. If marketed just right, it could be a smash hit for the company. He'd already begun toying with several ideas for slogans and thinking through how he'd like the interior to be photographed.

"She's quite the car," said a woman.

Maddux turned to see Rose Fuller standing next to him, camera slung around her neck. She took several pictures that required a flash. Maddux gently moved her to the side of the car and showed her where she'd get the best pictures.

"We want people to see the luxurious leather that we hope to make standard on all these vehicles when they finally hit the market," he said, urging her toward a particular spot.

"I didn't realize Opel was attempting to compete with Mercedes," she said.

"We're not," he said. "We're trying to be another viable option for car buyers in this market, an option for people with expensive tastes but who lack deep pockets."

"Can I quote you on that?" Rose asked as she pulled a notepad from her purse.

He glanced down at the tag dangling from her neck. "I didn't realize you were here as a journalist."

"Unlike you, I can more easily adapt to the situation. If they need me to be a journalist, I can be a journalist. But I promise they don't really want me writing anything that anyone else would read."

"Writing isn't your thing?"

"I can barely spell the word *two* correctly. And that makes it difficult when three differently spelled words all sound the same. Fortunately, spelling wasn't an important component for engineers wanting to join the CIA."

Maddux nodded. "So, you're here on official business?"

"I'm scoping out a few cars here, trying to see which ones might be the best to modify for our agents."

"Modify?"

She nodded. "I know sometimes you guys need cars that do more than just go fast. I've got several ideas I want to try out, but I don't want to build something from scratch."

"If you're going to modify one for me, make it a Mercedes-Benz."

Rose chuckled. "First of all, you're not quite an important enough agent for me to begin modifying cars for. And second, even if you were, I wouldn't send you out in one of those cars. The idea of being a secret agent is to blend in with the surroundings and avoid drawing attention to yourself. Driving a Mercedes-Benz doesn't accomplish that objective."

"Did anyone ever tell you that you're good at snuffing out dreams? I'm going to call you the Dream Crusher."

She smiled. "I crush the dreams of men every day, particularly the ones who think I might go out on a date with them." She paused, scanned the room, and then winked at him. "Fortunately for you, you're not in that category."

He furrowed his brow. "So you don't think I want to go out with you? From what you've told me, that's taboo in the agency."

"We'll have to discuss this some other time—over a glass of wine."

"I'm very confused right now."

She patted him on the back. "That's the point. The less you understand, the better. That can be a woman's greatest strength."

Maddux looked around at the throng of photographers still huddled around the Opel GT, snapping photos and ogling over the car.

"Perhaps you should snap some pictures if you want everyone to believe you're a real journalist."

She shrugged. "I've already taken all the photos I need. However, there is something I wanted to show you before I leave."

"Oh? What is it?"

"This," she said, handing him a grainy black-and-white picture. "I found it while doing some snooping a few days ago."

"Snooping for what? And who is this?"

"Look closely."

Maddux brought the photograph close to his face and studied the image for a moment before gasping.

"Is that really him?" he asked.

She nodded.

"It's recent," he said. "I can tell by the car."

Maddux looked back down at the picture again. It depicted his father leaning against a Corvette.

"These cars just arrived over here in Europe, so he might still be here," Maddux said. "Did you find out anything else about him?"

She shook her head. "Nope. Just that. I found it in a folder with his name on it."

"And the rest of it was empty?"

"Yeah, and I know this doesn't get you any closer to the truth about your father and what happened to him, but at least you know *something*."

A smile flashed across Maddux's face.

"I know he's still alive and the CIA has been keeping an eye on him. That much is for sure. So the next time

Pritchett tries to spin a new tale, I'll mention the photo and remind him that I know the truth about my father's existence. If anything, it'd be fun to watch him squirm."

Rose took a deep breath. "Trust me," she said, "you don't want to see him squirm because usually it results in him settling his nerves by destroying those who disagree with him. It's never pretty."

"Pritchett promised to tell me more."

"And I'm sure he will when he's ready to do it. But in the meantime, you need to keep your head down and complete your missions. That's the only way to stay in his good graces. If you don't stay on Pritchett's good side, there will be a steep price to pay, one that involves you losing access to every piece of history connecting your dad to the CIA."

"Can you tell me anything else about my father?"

Rose shook her head. "You've got everything I could find, I promise. I'm afraid that you're on your own from here on out."

A man charged up to Maddux and shook his hand vigorously, ending the conversation with Rose.

"As I live and breathe—John Hambrick," the man said. "You don't look like you've aged a day since I saw you last."

"And when was that?" Maddux asked cautiously.

"You don't remember?" the man asked before stopping and glancing down at Maddux's nametag.

Maddux followed the man's eyes.

"Oh, I'm sorry," the man said. "I've confused you with someone else."

He spun on his heels and walked in the opposite direction.

"No, wait," Maddux said.

But the man didn't turn around. He slipped into the sea of journalists moving on to the next auto manufacturer's grand unveiling of a car destined for mass production.

"Did you hear that?" Maddux asked.

Rose nodded. "He thought you were someone else. Happens all the time to me. If I had a nickel for every time some man stopped me in the street and asked me if anyone ever told me I look like Audrey Hepburn . . ."

Maddux stepped back and looked at Rose again.

"I can see that, though I think your eyes are much prettier," he said.

"Your attempts at flattery are wasted, remember? We're considered co-workers and aren't supposed to fraternize."

Maddux shrugged. "Right now you're a journalist trying to get the money shot on my new Opel GT that's going to be the next big thing in Europe, mark my word. And I think a little flirting won't do any harm."

"Trust me," she said. "They're always watching us, especially at events like this."

"Well, maybe we should return to the topic at hand and discuss how come that man is the second person in the last two weeks, not to mention the second person on as many continents, to tell me they thought I looked like somebody named John Hambrick."

"Coincidence?"

"I think not. That's too strange."

"Maybe John Hambrick had a common face, just like yours."

"You sure know how to pump up a guy's ego."

Rose laughed. "That's probably why I'm still single, along with the fact that I prefer tinkering with electronic toys rather than toying with men."

Maddux glanced at his watch. The exhibit hall would remain open for another half hour, yet he wondered if anyone would become suspicious if he detained Rose any longer. He enjoyed their banter, both playful and serious.

Before he could ask her another question, a man in a suit approached and asked, "I need you to come with me."

Maddux studied him closely. "I don't even know who you are, Mr.—"

"Agent Wright, of the CIA," he said.

Maddux turned toward Rose.

"I know him," she said. "He's legit."

"Okay," Maddux said. "Where are we going?"

Wright took up a position behind them and gently nudged them toward the door.

"Mr. Maddux, you've got a long ride ahead of you," he said.

"What's going on?"

"I'll tell you more outside."

Wright led them through the crowd and down a long hallway which eventually spilled onto a loading dock at the back of the exhibit hall. He strode up to the first of two black sedans and opened the door, gesturing for them to get inside.

Maddux moved out of the way for Rose to get in first, but Wright held up his hand to stop her.

"You're needed back at headquarters," he said, pointing at the other car. "Just Mr. Maddux in this one."

She backed up and moved out of the way for Maddux. "I'll see you when you return," she said.

"I want that fancy car," he said.

She chuckled and sighed before getting into her designated car.

Maddux had barely stepped into the vehicle behind Rose's before Wright slammed the door behind him and then slipped into the front seat.

"Will you tell me what's going on?" Maddux asked.

"There's a defector at the border that you need to retrieve for us," Wright said. "He goes by the name of Otto Voss. He's a former scientist for the Nazis, but he needs our help."

"We're going to help a Nazi escape?"

"A Nazi scientist, to be exact," Wright said. "And we're not doing anything. You are going to get him back to Bonn along with the rest of his family—and we're going to fly him to the U.S. where he could help our Army research team."

"If you insist," Maddux said.

"No, Mr. Maddux, I don't have to insist. I tell you what to do and you do it. Is that understood?"

Maddux nodded. "Loud and clear."

Wright handed Maddux a packet. "That contains all the information you'll need to successfully retrieve and return Mr. Voss and his family to Bonn, where they'll be transferred back to the U.S. The driver here will take you to your car. Good luck, Mr. Maddux."

Wright slipped out of the car and then joined Rose in her vehicle while Maddux opened the packet and started reading.

What have I gotten myself into now?

SIX MONTHS LATER

NEW YORK CITY

VOSS SMILED TO HIMSELF as he stepped off the train and onto the subway platform. He hustled up the steps toward his Brooklyn apartment. With a polite nod, Voss said hello to a few neighbors in the building who were heading out. They kindly replied and kept moving. Voss remained surprised at how well Ingrid and Astrid had settled into their new home in the U.S., particularly his daughter. A new culture, a new country—and no familiar faces. And yet Astrid was thriving. Voss entered his home to find her playing a board game with a friend from school.

"Hi, Papa," she said. "Would you like to play Candyland with us?"

"Candyland? That sounds fun," Voss said. "Maybe in a few minutes after I speak with your mother."

Voss put his briefcase down and ventured toward his bedroom, where through a cracked door he could see telltale signs of Ingrid's activities that day. Two columns of shoe boxes stacked three high sat on the end of the bed. He pushed the door open and walked in.

"Ingrid?" he called.

No answer.

"Ingrid? Where are you?"

Another long moment of silence before he heard the clicking of heels on the bathroom tile. Shortly after, she walked into the room and threw her hands out. "So, Otto, what do you think?"

Ingrid wore a sequined red dress, accented by a pair of red heels. She turned her head toward him slightly, showing off a pair of dangling earrings.

"Do we have reservations tonight that I forgot about?" he asked.

She stamped her foot. "Otto, how many times are you going to say the wrong thing? Do I need to tell you what you need to say every time?"

Voss closed his eyes and shuttered. When he opened his eyes, he gazed at Ingrid and smiled. "Let me try that again."

"Yes, please do."

"Ingrid, you look beautiful. One might even say stunning."

"Would you say stunning?"

Voss nodded vigorously. "Of course. How could I say anything else?"

Ingrid's face dropped. "Either you still need help in the nuances of the English language, or we still have a lot of work to do with you."

She patted him on the face and slipped out of the shoes. "As the Americans say, I'm going to whip you into shape."

"Well, you certainly seem to be fitting into American culture just fine with all those shoes. If there's one thing

I've noticed about American women, it's that they just can't have enough shoes."

"Since when did you become so observant about women's fashion?"

"I can't really discuss it, but it's work related."

"Work related?" she said with a laugh before sitting on the edge of the bed and putting on a different pair of shoes. "I didn't know you came here to be a cobbler. I thought you were still working as a scientist."

"I am," he said. "But I can't really discuss it. It's kind of a secret project."

"Flying shoes, perhaps?" she said, arching her eyebrows. "You are a physicist. I can't think of anything else you'd be using shoes for while working with the Americans."

"You know I can't discuss this with you, don't you?"

"Oh, what is it going to hurt? Are you afraid I'm going to blurt out everything I know to the lady who sells me these shoes?"

"It's nothing that should get your dander up," he said, bristling as he loosened his tie.

"I think you know more about American culture than you're letting on," she said. "You certainly know the lingo—and the American pastime of shutting down a woman."

"I'm not shutting you down, Ingrid. I simply can't talk about it."

"Can't or don't want to?"

"Both."

Ingrid slammed her shoes into the box. "You are an impossible man, Otto. Impossible, I tell you."

"Fine. If you must know, I only know about the

shoes because the project I'm working on has teamed me up with a woman who I've happened to notice wears a different pair of shoes almost every day to work. Then I started to notice all the women who work at the lab must own a closet that's only full of shoes."

"There are women at your lab?"

"Just a few," he said. "They are more like lab assistants."

"And what is this project you're working on?"

He slumped into a chair in the corner of the room. "You are relentless."

She moved across the room and started massaging his back. "Otto, your secrets are safe with me. I think you know that by now. Besides, it's not like I don't know the biggest secret you have—the one about you spying for the motherland."

"I'm not spying for Russia or Czechoslovakia," he said. "I'm spying for you and Astrid."

"And if you didn't have to spy?"

"I wouldn't. I just want to have a normal life."

Ingrid sighed and walked over to the dresser. She collected an envelope and handed it to her husband.

"This won't make you feel any more normal," she said. "Instead, it will only remind you of the situation we're currently in, which is as far from normal as we can get."

"What is this?"

"I don't know," she said. "I didn't open it."

Voss looked at her, cocking his head to one side. "You? You didn't open this? My wife who wants to know every dark secret that I know? You didn't try to peek or hold it up to the light and see if you could make out some of the words?"

She shook her head. "I had a busy day. What can I say?"

"I find that hard to believe, despite how many shoes you bought."

"It came just before you arrived home. Someone slid it under the door. I raced into the hallway, but I didn't see anyone."

Voss stood. "Okay, I'll go read this in my study."

"Why not read it here?" she said, stopping him with an embrace and a kiss. "I'll rub your back while you read it."

He turned sideways and moved past her. "I'll just read it in my office if it's all the same to you. There are some things I'd rather you not know so it keeps you out of trouble."

"How thoughtful of you, dear," she said with a smirk.

"It's for your own good," he said, waving the envelope as he eased into the hallway.

Once Voss entered his study, he shut the door behind him and settled into his reading chair. Before he sat down, he pulled out a folded up sheet of paper and then opened it. An address was hastily scrawled, but Voss could make out all the letters. He knew exactly where it was—and who it belonged to, even though there was no accompanying name. Ever since he'd arrived in New York, he'd been seeking this small piece of information, one he thought he'd never get.

But when he met Alice Buxley, the woman who served as a liaison between his office and the CIA, he seized his chance. The truth is, Alice was the woman whose shoes he'd noticed. He created the story about his co-worker to keep Ingrid from bombarding him with an avalanche of questions. She would want to know everything about a secret CIA woman.

If anything, Voss felt somewhat guilty about his overtly flirtatious approach with Alice. He even went out for drinks with her once, making up another lie about having to work late for Ingrid. But over the course of a couple of months, Voss managed to win Alice's trust— so much so that he gained the confidence he needed to ask her for all the information she had on a man named Gregory Mikhailov. Voss reflected how fortunate he was to never cross any marital lines to secure the information, even though he did see plenty of blurred lines in his method.

He looked down at the sheet of paper and smiled while he committed the address to memory. The fruit of his labor now rested firmly in his mind.

Voss's next order of business was to open the mysterious envelope. He had an idea of what he might find but hoped he was wrong.

He wasn't.

The letter was written in code, but one he understood all too well. Voss interpreted the message from Mikhailov. The StB official wanted to know any information that Voss had collected, along with a reason why he'd only contacted him once after landing in the U.S. Mikhailov explained the importance of transmitting information back in a timely manner and how if he didn't hear from Voss within a week, harsh action would be taken, which explicitly mentioned that outing him as a spy would be an option.

But Voss had already planned to give Mikhailov

exactly what he wanted before giving him a little something extra. However, Voss's bonus wouldn't be something Mikhailov would appreciate or ever want. Yet, the message needed to be sent.

Voss opened his hutch and began composing a note for Ingrid. He knew she'd be angry and upset initially but would eventually understand. His family's situation would improve. From Voss's perspective, anything was better than pretending to befriend kindhearted souls in a foreign land only to stab them in the back and spill all their secrets to an opposing force hell bent on wreaking havoc. Voss likened the experience to being trapped in a prison without bars. He'd never be able to escape the clutches of either side. Americans would see him as a traitor for simply agreeing to the plot; Russians would cast him as a defector for turning on them. Either way, one side would be dissatisfied and exact the type of revenge reserved for the worst of the worst. Surveying his options, Voss believed the few he had were more about choosing the lesser of two evils.

Later that night, while Ingrid took an evening shower, he quickly packed a bag and stashed it in his study. After Ingrid was sound asleep, Voss crept out of bed, grabbed his bag, and walked to a busy intersection where he caught a cab for the airport. Once there, he bought a ticket for Berlin on the redeye and was likely halfway across the Atlantic before his wife woke up and realized he was gone.

Voss called Ingrid once he landed to tell her what he was doing, though he was careful not to divulge all the details. In his effort to protect her from any scrutiny, he figured that the less she knew, the better.

"You're where?" she asked.

"In Berlin," Voss said.

"What on earth for? What about your jobs?"

"I needed to take care of a few things."

"And you didn't think I deserved to know this ahead of time?"

Voss sighed. "I can't discuss all the details with you, but it was a sudden decision based on some correspondence I received. I needed to speak to a colleague in Prague, and it wasn't something I could do any other way than in person."

"Don't do it," Ingrid said. "Just come home. Find another way to talk to him. If you go back . . ."

Her words hung in the air, the implication of what she meant didn't need to be said. Voss understood clearly. However, he also understood that Ingrid's limited knowledge about the situation was why she felt the way she did.

"I know who did it," Voss said.

"Did what?"

"Beat you."

"How did you—?"

"It doesn't matter. Any man who beats you and terrorizes Astrid the way he did—"

"No one terrorized Astrid," she said, cutting her husband's answer short. "I told you that. She was just scared."

"That's terrorizing. I heard her screams. And while they may have never laid a finger on her, that moment will stick with her for the rest of her life. She'll never be able to shake hearing her father beaten like I was."

"She's moved on," Ingrid said. "She's adjusted to her

life in America and is playing with dolls and new friends. It's the life you always wanted for her. She's happy. Now, don't mess everything up by trying to be a hero."

"I'm not trying to be a hero. I only want revenge— and the freedom that comes along with it."

"What are you going to do, Otto?"

Otto took a deep breath, exhaling slowly. He rubbed his forehead as considered his response.

"Well, Otto, are you going to answer me or not?" Ingrid said, her impatience growing with each passing second of silence.

"Don't worry, Ingrid. Everything will be fine in a few days. I promise. I'll call you when it's done."

* * *

AN HOUR LATER, Voss was sitting in the apartment of StB agent, Linus Müller. Müller worked at the Czechoslovakian embassy in Berlin, serving as a liaison for business leaders inquiring about the possibility of establishing operations inside the Czech border. The position allowed Müller the opportunity to dig deep into the businesses for official government purposes, helping him avoid scrutiny for his investigative work. With global markets expanding, the Eastern bloc nations—and even Russia—understood that in order to remain a world power, they couldn't ignore the potential economic partnerships blossoming everywhere. To build an impenetrable fortress when it came to commerce was a mistake destined to impoverish their nations. Yet the StB also felt it was vital to understand who they were doing business with. Müller also made for a convenient contact for StB spies operating behind enemy lines.

"What kind of intelligence did you bring me?"

Müller asked as he packed tobacco into his pipe.

"We're going to talk this openly here?" Voss replied. "If there's one thing I've learned about the Americans, it's that—"

"Enough," Müller said. "Come with me."

Müller stood and walked across the room, motioning for Voss to follow. They went downstairs into the basement, Müller allowing Voss to go first before closing the door. The lock clicked, and Voss swallowed hard.

"Don't worry," Müller said. "I don't keep any of my trophies down here. It's too messy."

Voss tried to ignore the comment, though it plagued his psyche as he listened to his host speak.

"Now, if you're worried about such talk, this room should put you at ease," Müller said. "This room was reinforced with steel plates—all four walls along with the floor and ceiling. No one can drill into this room to listen, and there are no known devices that can pick up a soft conversation through this type of fortress."

"So as long as you don't yell at me, we're safe?" Voss asked.

Müller glared at Voss. "Why would I yell at you?"

"No reason, but I wanted to make sure."

"Very well then. Please carry on and answer the question I asked you: What kind of intelligence did you bring me?"

Voss dug into his pocket and produced a coin.

"So, you brought me American quarters?" Müller asked. "I'm quite familiar with U.S. currency."

"It's what's inside them that you'll find most interesting."

"And what might that be?"

"Microdots which contain most of what I've learned while serving with the U.S. Army scientists."

Müller held his hand out. "Excellent. Let's have a look."

Voss shook his head. "I'm sorry, but I need to deliver these in person to Mikhailov. He told me not to trust anyone."

Müller lit his pipe and paced around the basement. "So, let me get this straight," Müller said. "You came to me for help—me, an StB agent. Yet you won't show me what you found."

"I have my orders," Voss said.

"Perhaps you do, but I also have mine. How do I know you're not a double agent? And that what's in those quarters aren't microdots but instead are listening devices you're going to use against your own country?"

"You'll have to trust me, I guess," Voss said. "Besides, I'm just doing what Mikhailov told me to do. And I always follow orders, always."

"That's not what I heard," Müller quipped. "However, you're definitely going to need to let me see them because I can't request any protection for you if I can't verify your intelligence."

"Then I guess we're at a standstill because I will not budge."

"Perhaps I can convince you to change your mind."

"As the Americans like to say, you'll be barking up the wrong tree."

Müller inhaled the sweet tobacco smell from his pipe and exhaled slowly. "I don't even know what that means."

"It means that you'll be embarking on a fruitless

journey, one destined to fail."

"If I'm going to help you, I need to bark up the right tree then."

Voss shoved the coins back into his pocket and sighed. "Mikhailov told me to trust no one," Voss said. "I'm afraid I'll have to find my own way there."

He turned and started to walk up the stairs.

"Wait," Müller said. "Let me make a phone call." He walked across the room to a phone sitting on the desk and dialed a number. Holding out the receiver to Voss, Müller said, "Someone wants to speak with you."

Voss took the phone and pressed it to his ear. No one had answered as he heard two more rings before someone picked up.

"Mikhailov," the man said.

"Mikhailov? Gregory Mikhailov?" Voss said cautiously.

"Yes. Who is this? You sound like Otto Voss."

"This is Otto. I'm with one of your friends from the embassy. You told me to never reveal any classified information to anyone other than you. However, he refuses to help me unless I show him what I have."

"What are you doing in Germany?"

"I received your note," Voss said. "And the information I have is too important to be delivered by any method other than in person."

"I see."

"How would you like me to proceed?"

"Everyone is following protocol as instructed," Mikhailov said. "However, I need to know that you're sincere in your intentions."

Voss grunted. "You do not trust me, yet you send

me on the most dangerous of missions to infiltrate an impenetrable group of people. And I return with valuable information for you. Yet, you don't believe me. If I were you—"

"Watch your next words very carefully, Otto. In case you have forgotten, it's very easy for me to report your traitorous ways to the country that has so generously welcomed you in with open arms."

"Your threats are becoming tiresome."

"They are not threats," Mikhailov said. "They are promises, and if you do have valuable information for me, I suggest you allow my friend to inspect it before providing you with a way to meet me."

"Very well," Voss said. "I'll give it to him."

"That would please me very much. Now, let me talk to your friend."

Voss handed the phone back to Müller, who spoke briefly with Mikhailov, mostly with head nods and affirmative responses. When Müller hung up, he turned and looked at Voss.

"I need to see your intelligence, per Mikhailov's orders."

Voss held out his hand where a quarter sat in the center of his palm. "I think this should satisfy all your prerequisites."

Müller snatched the quarter and finagled the coin open. He tapped it several times until a microdot fell into his hand. "Sorry about the trouble, but protocol is protocol. And in my world, protocol is everything."

Müller hustled across the room and placed the dot on a viewing device, studying several pages for a few minutes. He proceeded to turn the machine off before marching back across the room to the phone. After Müller dialed a number, Voss listened in on the conversation.

"It is legitimate," Müller said, followed by another series of head nods and a few final parting words: "Consider it done."

"Follow me back upstairs," Müller said as he turned to Voss. "We have to get you ready for your journey back across the border."

MADDUX AWOKE AT 3:30 A.M. to vigorous knocking. He grabbed his gun and crept toward his front door. For a moment, he forgot he was living in Germany and feared Carolyn Wallace, his nosy neighbor from New York, would confront whoever was attempting to beat down his door.

Thank God there are no Carolyns in my apartment here.

He peeped through the hole and relaxed once he recognized his visitor. Maddux went through the routine of sliding the chain to the side and unlocking the deadbolt before he opened the door. Standing in the hallway was Barbara Carson.

"Nice robe," Carson said, running the back of her hand along Maddux's fluffy housecoat.

Maddux stared at his CIA colleague for a moment, still trying to wake up. "What brings you here at this time of night?"

She shot him a furtive glance and answered in a low voice. "We're not going to have this conversation in the hall."

Maddux stuck his head out of the doorway and looked in both directions before gesturing for her to come inside. "Sorry about that," he said as he shut the door. "I'm still a little out of sorts. So, what's this all about?"

"You need to quickly pack a suitcase. We need to get on the road."

"What for? Where are we going?"

"Get enough clothes for three days," she said. "I'll fill you in once we're on our way."

Fifteen minutes later, Maddux was fully dressed and toting a packed suitcase out of his apartment with Barbara.

"Would you mind telling me what's going on now?" Maddux asked once they were both safely in Barbara's car.

"Do you remember that scientist you picked up a few months ago near the Czech border?" she said as she twisted the key in the ignition.

"How could I forget?" Maddux said. "That was my first mission here. Nice guy with a fine family."

"I'd be careful about making quick judgments in this business, if I were you."

"Is that what this is about?"

Barbara eased onto the gas as she checked her surroundings. "Otto Voss, the scientist you escorted back, was placed with a secret group of scientists who were working on some highly classified projects. Turns out Voss was a plant from the Russians, and now he's heading back to Prague to deliver all the secrets he uncovered."

"But we know where he is?"

"We have an idea of where he's going based off a phone call we intercepted yesterday between a Czechoslovakian embassy staff member named Linus Müller and a high-ranking official in the Czech StB, Gregory Mikhailov. The intelligence we gathered suggested that Voss was with Müller and that he was going to help their spy back across the border."

"Is someone following them?"

"Not exactly," Barbara said. "However, a few months ago we identified several spies sneaking back and forth across the Czech-German border. We tracked their movements and were able to pinpoint the safe locations they moved between and how long they spent at each place. Now, we're able to tag certain spies that follow the same route as well as set traps for them coming and going."

"So, where are we going?"

"A little bed and breakfast outside of Stadelhofen, a few hours west of the Czech border."

"Voss is expected to be there tomorrow?"

"Oh, no," she said. "That location contains the fewest number of watchers, according to our reports. Voss won't arrive for a couple days, but in order for us to maintain a good cover, we need to get to Stadelhofen well before he does."

"We might stick out like sore thumbs, don't you think? A man and a woman traveling on business to Prague?"

Barbara chuckled. "You think we're going as business partners?"

He nodded. "Well, what is the plan then?"

"We're newlyweds, honey," she said, placing her hand

on Maddux's leg and giving it a squeeze. "And now we're going on our honeymoon."

Maddux gently nudged Barbara's hand off his leg.

"I'm not really into all the romantic stuff," he said.

"You strike me as a quick learner, Maddux. I'm sure you'll be debonair by the end of the weekend."

He sighed. "I didn't say I don't know how to do it. It's just not something I'm into. I can do it if I must."

She looked at him admiringly, lingering for a few seconds before returning her eyes to the road. "My god, how do you do it?"

"Do what?" Maddux asked.

"Exist?"

Maddux glanced at her and furrowed his brow. "What are you talking about?"

She smiled and kept her focus on the road. "Based on your response, you must be completely unaware of the effect that your deep smooth voice and chiseled body has on women."

"I'm not really comfortable with this conversation," Maddux said. "I've never heard a woman speak like this."

Barbara laughed. "It's the sixties, Maddux. Where have you been? Women are no longer staying tucked out of sight. Prim and proper is a fossilized idea. You really should get out more."

"Maybe I haven't noticed because I'm not interested."

She scowled and shot a quick glance at him. "You're not—"

"Oh, no," he said, shaking his head vigorously. "It's just that the pain of breaking a woman's heart was too much for me to bear. After I got divorced, I vowed to avoid getting myself into such situations. It's better for everyone."

"Let me tell you something, Maddux. You can't always control the hearts that you break. Some women will swoon and fall for you even if you don't give them the time of day. And sometimes when you ignore them, that can make the situation even worse. Women's hearts are curious in that way."

"I guess I can fake it for a few days," he said. "Just remember, this wasn't part of my training. I spent most of my time learning how to shoot, analyze situations, and extract information from hostiles."

"You'll have plenty of opportunities to implement your training," she said. "But when it comes to the newlywed cover, just follow my lead. You'll be fine."

* * *

JUST IN TIME FOR BREAKFAST, Barbara and Maddux pulled up to the Stadelhofen bed and breakfast, Gaestehaus Hellwig. Several guests were seated in the dining area and were already enjoying a generous breakfast. The sausage piled on a dish in the center of the table excited Maddux. He nearly blurted out something in English but remembered before blowing his cover.

"*Frühstückswurst*," he said with a smile.

One of the men turned around and held up a piece of sausage.

"*Gut*," the man said.

Maddux and Barbara meandered over to the receptionist area, which was left unattended. Barbara rang the bell, which resulted in the waitress scurrying over to speak with them.

"I'm sorry," the woman said in German. "My husband

and I run this bed and breakfast, and we do everything around here."

"I understand," Barbara responded in her best German. "My husband and I need to get a room for a couple nights."

"You two are quite fortunate since I just had a gentleman cancel his stay for tomorrow," the woman said. "Otherwise, you would've only been able to stay tonight."

"It looks like our honeymoon is off to a great start."

The woman smiled at them. "You're honeymooners?"

Barbara nodded.

"And you didn't plan for the honeymoon?"

Barbara leaned in and whispered. "We didn't even plan for the marriage, but that's what I love about this man. He is so spontaneous."

The woman's eyes widened. "Well, we do have one room that is clean, and you can place your luggage in there now if you so wish and join us for breakfast."

"Sounds delightful, doesn't it, honey?" Barbara asked Maddux.

"Certainly, dear," he said, leaning over and kissing Barbara on the cheek.

The woman gave them the room rate and waited while Maddux dug into his wallet, fished out the money, and handed it to her.

"Excellent," the woman said, exchanging the money for a key. "It's on the second floor, last door on your left. And it's the only room with its own private bathroom."

They thanked her and returned outside where Maddux retrieved their suitcases and lugged them upstairs. Barbara immediately began to set up her things on the counter. Maddux, however, scanned the room, looking at the queen bed pushed up against the far wall.

"This should be interesting," he said.

"Oh, don't be such a prude," Barbara said. "If you're going to be a spy, you need to learn that sometimes the call of duty supersedes your personal desires and preferences. There are moments when a spy must simply do what a spy needs to do. And for you, that means acting like we're not only married but madly in love."

Barbara approached him slowly and then gave him a kiss on the cheek.

Maddux withdrew and eyed her closely. "Our cover is about how we act in public, not behind closed doors."

She searched his face for a moment. "If I didn't know any better, Maddux, I'd guess you do have the hots for someone else."

Maddux spun on his heels and walked toward the bathroom. "I need to freshen up before we go downstairs and eat breakfast."

Maddux washed his face and emerged from the bathroom to find Barbara in the middle of trying to slip on a new dress. The back hung open, her blond hair tied into a tight bun.

"Would you mind zipping me up?" she asked without turning around.

Maddux obliged without saying a word.

"You can be cold toward me in here, but out there, you better get into your cover quickly," she said.

Maddux slumped into a chair and put on his shoes.

"If Otto Voss happens to show up early, I need to know what the end game of this mission is," he said. "Are we simply supposed to drag him back to Bonn and let Pritchett and company deal with him?"

"Not exactly."

"What is that supposed to mean?"

She hiked her skirt up just enough to adjust the holster hugging her right thigh. "It means that you better be a swift grave digger."

Maddux jumped to his feet. "You mean we're supposed to kill him if he doesn't agree."

Barbara let out an exasperated breath. "We don't work for a charity in case you've forgotten. And our mark isn't exactly someone we want running around with Russians, considering all that he now knows. Make sense?"

"Yeah, but—"

"There are no buts in our assignment. We try to turn him through persuasive means. And if that doesn't work—"

"What kind of means?"

"The kind of means you've been trained in. Besides, his wife and daughter are still in the U.S. That alone should be all the persuasion he needs."

"And how quickly is he expected to give us an answer?"

"We're not gonna let him sleep on it, if that's what you're suggesting," she said. "He's either in or out—and he'll have to make his decision in a prompt manner."

Maddux took a deep breath and walked over to the window, scanning the mountains towering in the distance.

"This is what you signed up for," Barbara said. "This is what it means to keep state secrets. It's a dirty business and sometimes you have to play by a set of dirty rules."

"But I don't want to lose my soul in the process."

"Better than losing your life," she said as she tugged on his sleeve. "Now, let's go. There are some *frühstück-swursts* in the dining room with your name on them."

Maddux knew his partner was right, though it bothered him. He'd already ventured way too far down the path to turn back.

"I'm not going to lose my soul or my life," he said as he moved toward the door. "There are ways to get what you want without stooping down into the mud with your enemy. You can rise above it."

"Those are some naïve statements, Maddux. Wait until you've wallowed in the muck before making such bold declarations. You might find that sometimes there's only one way through."

Maddux turned and winked at Barbara before placing his hand on the doorknob. "There's always more than one way through."

VII

THE NEXT EVENING, VOSS pulled up to the Gaestehaus Hellwig and took his suitcase out of the trunk. Dragging his luggage into the receptionist area, he set it down before ringing the bell. An elderly woman wobbled out of the back, greeting him with a smile.

"You must be Mr. Weber," she said.

He smiled and nodded.

"We've been expecting you," she said. "You are our last customer of the night."

She proceeded to give him all the ground rules for the property as well as information about the next morning's breakfast.

"Since you won't be staying long, I will skip the part about what time our delicious dinners are served. However, you're still here in time to enjoy our own biergarten tonight. We only serve drinks and will be open for another hour."

Voss thanked her and headed to his room. Fifteen minutes later, he decided to unwind with a pint of beer. He purchased a drink and sat down.

In the corner of the room, an elderly gentleman sat

on a stool and played an accordion softly. Based off the kiss he received from the lady who checked Voss in, he assumed the two were married and owned the business. He glanced around the outdoor deck nestled in the forest. One gentleman sat alone in the corner but quickly vacated his table after finishing his beer. The only other patrons were a couple, who were quite affectionate with one another.

Voss considered the road ahead of him. He'd cross the border the next morning and wouldn't have to continue watching over his shoulder. He couldn't believe his good luck thus far, avoiding even a hint of any allied spies. Voss attributed that fact to the special care taken by the StB to create a secure route. Based on what Linus Müller had said, Voss wondered if any of the allied spies even knew such a route existed. Every person had been vetted, though plenty of people along the route died under suspicious circumstances. However, he assumed the allies hadn't put it together yet. Voss took a deep breath and then a long pull on his mug. He hadn't felt this good since he'd returned to Germany.

When Voss got up to get a second pint, he noticed a man sitting in the shadows. The man had a hat pulled down low across his face. He gave Voss a one-finger salute, touching the brim of his hat with his index finger.

Voss scanned the room, hoping no one noticed. The bartender was busy cleaning glasses while neither the accordion player or the love-struck couple seated nearby noticed.

For the next half hour, Voss drank his beer and tapped his feet to the gentle music emanating from the old man's instrument. Voss glanced at his watch and decided he'd stay for another few minutes before retiring for the evening. He spent the rest of his time creating a mental checklist of all the things he needed to accomplish before striking off early in the morning. Voss became so lost in his thoughts that he didn't notice either the man in the corner or the couple get up and walk out of the biergarten.

The old man's music finally came to a halt, though it was the long pause that alerted Voss to the fact that the song was over. He stood and felt the cool breeze blowing through the woods. In the absence of accordion sounds, a cacophony of insects and amphibians filled the forest, all joined by the smooth rhythm of a trickling stream. Crickets chirped, bullfrogs bellowed. Voss, on the other hand, didn't make a sound, instead grinning ear to ear as he reveled in nature's orchestra.

He set his mug down and walked toward the exit. The great room was vacated and quiet, save the soft crackling of a dwindling flame in the fireplace. He settled into a chair and reflected on his journey. He missed Ingrid and Astrid so much he likened his longing to a searing pain. But he deemed this a worthwhile venture. He'd be free soon enough of all the cajoling and coercing, the threats and the lies. He considered disappearing into the southern hemisphere, perhaps taking up residence as a professor at a small university. His aspiration of greatness had long since vanished along with the innocence of his scientific discipline. No longer was physics about understanding matter and motion in space and time; physics had now become a place to gain an upper hand in war. And Voss wanted no part of it.

Voss closed his eyes and smiled, picturing himself in a small city in South America. He saw Astrid biting into a juicy mango against the backdrop of his luscious yard dotted with banana trees. Ingrid sat on the porch, wearing a flower in her hair while sipping a drink. A blue-and-yellow macaw perched atop his fence filled the air with its gurgling call. The vision served as motivation to push on even when he felt weary from the travel and constant tension of keeping his head on a swivel. Yet, his daydream ended abruptly when he felt a firm hand lock around the back of his neck.

"We need to talk," the man said.

Voss opened his eyes to see the man holding an index finger to his lips. Amidst the flickering flames that intermittently illuminated the man's face, Voss thought his captor looked familiar.

"Come with me," the man said.

Voss stood and walked with the man. Compliance with the demand wasn't Voss's first inclination, but the round object jammed into his back convinced him that any other option was foolish.

The man led Voss upstairs and into a room where a woman was seated on the bed as if awaiting their arrival.

"You?" Voss said, realizing he recognized the man. "Aren't you the same man who escorted me to the U.S. embassy when I declared my intentions to defect?"

"I am," Maddux said. "I'm here to make sure that you keep your promise."

"Promise? Promise to do what? What do you even think I'm doing here?"

"Have a seat," the woman said, pointing at the chair across the room. "We need to talk."

Voss complied but didn't waste any time voicing his objections. "I hope you know I'm being watched," he said. "This is very much endangering my mission."

"Your mission?" she asked. "And what exactly does your mission entail?"

"It's classified."

"Classified? By whose authority?" Maddux asked.

"I can't say," Voss said. "I'd tell you if I could, but I—"

"Barbara Carson," the woman said, extending her hand.

Voss ignored it.

"You might want to reconsider your position here. I'm here to help."

Voss huffed a sarcastic laugh through his nose. "Is that what you people are calling it these days—*help*?"

Crossing his arms, Maddux stood directly in front of Voss. "And while you might be on a mission, I need you to tell me right now who ordered it," Maddux said. "Something isn't right here."

Voss narrowed his eyes. "I'm afraid I can't do that."

"Well, you're either going to do that or you're going to explain to me where this came from," Maddux said as he held up a hollowed-out quarter used to store microdots.

Voss raised both hands, exposing the perspiration beading on his palms. "It's not what you think."

Maddux cocked his head back and glared down at Voss. "Then you better get to explaining quick because from where I stand this is treason. It's not exactly the best way to treat a country that rescued you from brutal taskmasters."

"It wasn't supposed to happen like this," Voss said.

"I-I only wanted to escape. But your country rejected me, and I was returned across the border."

"Rejected you?" Barbara asked. "I'm afraid you must be mistaken."

"No, I swear to you, it's true," Voss argued. "A man promised me a way out and then snuck me and my family across the border to a U.S. outpost. But the agents refused to take me and instead dropped me off back at the Czech border."

"Your name never appeared in any files at our offices in Bonn," Barbara said. "And our soldiers are required to file a report on anyone who even attempts to seek asylum in allied territory."

"I know it might sound convenient, but I used an alias, William Richards, you know, the famous Czech spy."

Barbara chuckled. "He's so famous, I've never heard of him."

"That's what they told me," Voss countered.

"Who told you that?"

"Gregory Mikhailov, my contact at the Czech StB."

Barbara arched her eyebrows. "*The* Gregory Mikhailov?"

Voss shrugged. "I guess. There's only one man I know there who works by that name."

Barbara clapped her hands, rubbing them together. "This is shaping up better than I imagined."

Maddux grunted. "As long as he's compliant and isn't trying to play us for fools."

"I've never heard of a William Richards," Barbara said. "You most likely fell for one of the StB's dirtiest tricks."

"What do you mean?" Voss asked.

"You likely never crossed any border or visited any U.S. Army outpost either," Barbara explained. "It was all a ruse just to get you to comply with their wishes."

She paced around the room and continued.

"I'm going to guess that Mikhailov asked you on more than one occasion to spy on the U.S. for him. And then when you declined, he threatened you. Not long after you felt threatened, you met a man who offered to take you across the border to safety, maybe even made you grand promises."

Mouth agape, Voss stared at Barbara.

"How do you know such things? That is exactly what happened."

Barbara sighed. "You're not the first person to fall for the StB's mind games. It's standard protocol for them."

"Yes, yes," Voss said. "So, I was tricked. I never wanted to leave my homeland, but I had to. And I never wanted to join in some damned fool mission for Mikhailov. I just wanted to live a peaceful life with my family and study physics, nothing more than that."

Maddux stroked his chin. "Yet, here you are with hollowed-out quarters filled with microdots containing U.S. secrets."

"It was only so I could get back into the country and appear legitimate, I swear to you." Voss buried his head in his hands, refusing to look up for several seconds.

"That's going a bit too far."

"I only showed them benign secrets," Voss said, "things I know the Russian's team of scientists know already."

"It's still treason, Otto," Barbara said. "There's still a price to pay, even for the slightest of indiscretions."

"No, no," Voss said. "Please. Show me mercy. I'll do anything you want. But you have to let me back in. Mikhailov has promised to ruin me if I don't give him this information. And he's expecting it now. He's promised to out me as a spy if I don't comply with his demands."

"And yet we know that you are and we are letting you live," Maddux said.

"You don't understand," Voss said. "Mikhailov has ways of reaching me. If he feels like I betrayed him, he will kill my wife and daughter, that much I am sure."

Barbara nudged Voss to the side and stepped forward, looking directly at him.

"I think I know what this is really about," she said. "I think you want revenge, don't you?"

Voss nodded. "I want to kill the sonofabitch who imprisoned my family, not with bars in a cell but with the kind of oppression I wouldn't wish upon my worst enemy. Death is far too great of a gift for Mikhailov."

"Just as I suspected," she said. "But I think there's a way for us to both emerge as winners in this situation."

"What if I disagree?"

"I'll shoot you in the head and bury your body in the woods," she said. "Mikhailov won't even bother to come look for you."

Voss scowled at her. "This is how you influence people to do what you want?"

She shrugged. "It works."

Maddux put his arm on Barbara's back. "What she means is that we will help you if you are willing to help us. We can't let you go until you agree to do so."

"That's much more diplomatic," Voss said.

"So, you'll help?" Maddux asked.

Voss nodded. "Not that you gave me much of a choice."

"I think we share some common goals," Maddux said. "It'd behoove us all to work together rather than tearing each other apart. We face a formidable enemy in Russia, and its end game is oppression."

Voss shook his head. "No, it's far worse than that."

Barbara took out a sheet of paper and scribbled down an address before handing it to Voss.

"When you arrive in Prague, make a discreet visit to this apartment. The gentleman who lives there will give you the necessary equipment you need to fulfill your mission for us. But don't even think about running. We will hunt you down and—"

Maddux held his hand up to Barbara.

"That's enough," he said. "He's already agreed to work with us. No need to make extraneous threats."

Barbara glanced at Maddux before returning her steely gaze on Voss. She tugged on the bottom of her blouse and sighed. "Fine, but I'm serious. These aren't just threats, they're—"

"Okay, Barbara. We understand."

"If what you say is true," Voss said, "then I don't require any coaxing. You've already said plenty to persuade me to join you. I want to see Mikhailov pay for what he did."

"Just stick to the plan and do what our contact in Prague says," Barbara said. "He'll make sure you won't be disappointed."

"And how will I contact you?" Voss asked.

"You won't," Maddux said. "We'll find you."

Voss nodded and then stopped. He searched Maddux's face for a moment and then held a long gaze.

"Is everything all right?" Maddux asked.

"You look familiar," Voss said.

"Well, I did help you escape into Germany a few months ago."

"No, that's not it. I know your face from somewhere else. I just can't place it right now."

"Unless you went to New York before you escaped, I doubt we've ever met," Maddux said.

"No, I'm never wrong about a face. I have a photographic memory. And I know I've seen you before."

Maddux's gaze bounced between Barbara and Voss. "I don't know what you're talking about."

Voss held up his index finger. "It'll come to me. It always does."

He quietly exited the room and contemplated where he might have seen Maddux before.

I know I've seen him somewhere.

VIII

THE NEXT AFTERNOON, Maddux ambled into Pritchett's office, where Barbara was already comfortably seated in one of two chairs directly across from their boss. After exchanging pleasantries, Maddux settled into his seat. He checked his watch and tapped his hands on the armrest, waiting for Pritchett to get down to business.

"Antsy, aren't we?" Pritchett asked in more of a matter-of-fact way.

"I still have work to catch up on, not to mention sleep," Maddux said. "That trip took a lot out of me."

Pritchett, who'd been perusing a report, closed the folder, pinning it to the desk with his hook.

"This job takes a lot out of all of us, but we must learn to recover quickly," Pritchett said, looking over the top of his glasses.

"Let's get down to business, shall we?" Maddux asked.

"Very well then," Pritchett said, reopening the file. "From what Agent Carson tells me, you had a productive trip."

Maddux nodded. "We were able to turn the asset, which was what you tasked us with. From that perspective, it was a rousing success."

"But?" Pritchett asked.

"But what?"

Barbara scooted forward in her chair and cast a sideways glance at Maddux. "He wants to know why it wasn't a success."

"What would give you that idea?" Maddux asked as he arched his eyebrows.

"You added a qualifier—from that perspective," Pritchett said. "You seem to imply that there was another perspective."

Maddux sighed. "I think the way he was initially approached, he would've said anything to give us the impression that he was going to comply. So I'm not convinced that he's going to follow through with his end of the bargain."

"What are you suggesting?" Barbara asked, glaring at Maddux.

"I'm not suggesting anything," Maddux said. "I just think we could've been more diplomatic from the beginning in an effort to win his trust as opposed to strong-arming him from the moment he walked into the room."

Pritchett chuckled and shook his head. "Barbara, do we need to have a talk about your tactics? This wouldn't be the first time you—"

"I don't need another talk," she said, crossing her arms. "I know what to do."

"Then why do you seem to have so much trouble doing what I ask?"

She shrugged. "I just wanted to make sure he knew who was in charge. Sometimes our targets require heavy persuasion, and I didn't feel like taking all night to get the job done."

"And in the process, you almost lost him, didn't you?" Pritchett asked.

"Everything worked out in the end, didn't it?"

"That remains to be seen," Pritchett said, straightening the stack of papers he'd removed from the file. "But I believe we'll weather this stormy part of our relationship with Mr. Voss. He'll come around. Besides, thanks to you, he knows that he has no other choice but to help us."

Barbara forced a smile. "Maybe my methods aren't so bad after all."

"Don't push your luck," Pritchett said.

She stood and exited her boss's office, but Maddux didn't move.

"Is there something you wanted to speak to me about?" Pritchett asked.

Maddux glanced over his shoulder before leaping to his feet and closing the door. "As a matter of fact, there is."

"Spill it, Maddux."

Maddux scanned the room, contemplating his next words. "I think I've been more than patient with you."

"I'm not sure I'm following."

"You said you'd give me more information about my father when you could. Whether clearance was an issue or just permission to tell me what I have a right to know, you've yet to tell me anything other than the fact that my father is alive. Where is he? What has he been doing all these years? Why did he disappear like he did? Those are questions that have nagged me for years, and you have the answers, but for some reason you're not telling me anything. I'm starting to feel like I'm being led along a path toward a very unsatisfying ending."

Pritchett raised both arms in a posture of surrender. "I understand your frustration, but my hands are tied right now."

"What's the agency afraid of? That I'll divulge the truth to the media? Unearth some secret program? Find out what he's really doing?"

"It's complicated and I wish I could tell you more, but I simply can't—at least, not right now."

"Well, this is starting to get old," Maddux said. "Otto Voss told me on the way home that I looked like someone he'd met before—and he wasn't referring to a few months ago. I heard the same thing from another guy in this department, calling me John Hambrick, and swearing I looked like him. Those are a couple of strange coincidences, don't you think?"

"Don't read too much into it," Pritchett said. "If I had a nickel for every time someone approached me and asked me if I was someone that they once knew who had a hook for a right hand, I'd be sitting in a Swiss chalet somewhere instead of in this office. People want to make human connections desperately—and sometimes we see things that simply aren't there."

Maddux shook his head. "I think this is different, and I think you know that."

"You also fall into that category, Maddux. You want to see something. You want to make that connection. Don't try so hard that you conjure up something that isn't really there."

"I'm not conjuring up anything. Other people are the ones telling me these things. It's not as if I'm going around asking everyone if I have a familiar face to them."

"Nevertheless, it's a fool's errand. I won't hold anything back regarding your father once I get the information *and* permission to tell you."

"And that's supposed to satisfy me?"

"I hope it will for now because that's all I can tell you. Just be patient, and you'll receive all the answers you're looking for. That much I can promise. Now, is there anything else you wanted to ask me?"

Maddux shook his head and stood. "That's all for now."

"Good," Pritchett said. "I'll let you know when your visas come through for Czechoslovakia."

"You're sending me to Prague?"

"We'll discuss all the details tomorrow, but that's the plan for now. Just go home and get some rest. You're going to need it for the assignment that awaits you."

Maddux nodded and exited Pritchett's office. Lost in a mental haze, Maddux tried to digest his conversation with Pritchett. *Am I being paranoid? Am I trying to see something that isn't there? Is Pritchett only saying that to keep me from digging into the truth about my father? Or does Pritchett know the truth and just doesn't want me wasting my time?*

Maddux's contemplation only led to more questions, not answers, which was what he craved the most. He walked down the hall, eyes glazed over, unable to see the agent right in front of him—until they bumped into one another.

"Sorry about that," the agent said as he took a step back and smoothed out the sides of his jacket.

"It's my fault," Maddux said. "I wasn't paying attention to where I was going."

The agent nodded and sidestepped Maddux before continuing down the hall.

Maddux exited the building before he dug into his pockets to feel for his wallet. He pulled it out along with a sheet of paper.

I don't remember putting this in my pocket.

Maddux unfolded the note and read it.

September 12, 1952. *Lidové noviny*

Maddux stuffed the note back in his pocket while a plethora of new questions flooded his mind. *Who put this in my pocket? And why? Does this have to do with my father?*

He had his hunches, but he wasn't sure about the answer to any of those questions. But that didn't matter. Maddux was going to start digging for answers as soon as he had a chance.

IX

MADDUX ENTERED HIS OFFICE at Opel the next morning, feeling refreshed for the first time in a week. The good night of sleep had done wonders for his outlook, though the nagging questions about his father hadn't subsided. Maddux forced himself to push them aside so he could concentrate on his upcoming mission, which consisted of a trip to Prague.

At 9:30 a.m., Maddux met with his department head, Peter Wilhelm, for what was supposed to be a discussion about the upcoming week's projects. But instead, the meeting turned into a briefing about a last-minute trip that required Maddux to travel to Prague. According to Wilhelm, a Czechoslovakian car manufacturer was searching for a partner in Germany—and Opel was looking to expand.

Maddux questioned why he was chosen for the opening salvo of talks with the Czech company. Wilhelm explained that the prospective client's primary concern wasn't the quality of the product but the way the cars would be marketed.

"We can handle all the financial issues and contractual

obligations that arise during this partnership," Wilhelm explained. "But we need you to assure them that our marketing of the vehicles will exceed all of their expectations. And there's no one better to do that than you."

Maddux shrugged. "If you say so."

He wondered how many hoops Pritchett had to jump through to arrange the meeting between Opel and the Czechs. Pritchett's miracle-working skills were legendary among CIA agents. Maddux just couldn't believe Pritchett could concoct viable scenarios on such a short notice to create a plausible cover.

"Be careful out there," Wilhelm said with a wink and a solemn nod.

"Will do, sir."

Maddux's relationship with the CIA wasn't a surprise to his company since the agency approached GM first about transferring him to Germany. While he didn't know all the details about their unique relationship, Maddux just knew that one existed. However, who knew what remained a mystery.

Following the meeting, Maddux changed his hat and jacket before utilizing an underground passageway to sneak out of his office and make his way to the CIA station. With KGB agents staking out European businesses with American ties, Maddux was trained that he could never be too careful. Upon entering his official workplace, he needed to remain there for the duration of the day unless he was running a lunchtime errand or grabbing a bite to eat. Anything else was sure to draw suspicion if he was being followed. And Maddux was certain that he was under the watchful eyes of the KGB. He'd yet to make any of their agents, but he could just feel it.

Before reaching Pritchett's office, Maddux bumped into Rose Fuller. Her eyes widened, and she cocked her head to one side upon recognizing him.

"Ed Maddux," she said. "Just the man I wanted to see."

He glanced at his watch. "I've got a meeting with Pritchett in ten minutes."

She waved dismissively. "He can wait because without me, your next mission will be doomed before it starts."

"I must be the last to know what all this mission entails."

"Fortunately, it doesn't matter. I'm going to give you what you need to make it a success. Now, follow me."

Maddux followed Rose down a long corridor and several flights of stairs until they reached her lab. A half dozen tables were mostly covered with electronic gadgetry, while pairs of technicians clad in white coats hovered over their equipment.

"Is this where all the magic happens?" Maddux asked.

"Magic is all about illusion," she said. "What we do here is called science. And I've got more science than you can handle."

She led him to a back corner of the room before pressing a button on the wall. The bookcase in front of them began to turn, creating a small doorway. She gestured toward the opening.

"Care to join me?" she asked.

"How could I refuse?"

Maddux squeezed through the tight entryway, which led to a cavernous garage. His mouth fell agape as he surveyed the luxury sports cars parked in long diagonal rows facing each other. An Alfa Romeo Type 33 Stradale on one side, a Ferrari Dino 206 GT on the other. A Jaguar E-Type Coupe Series 1 positioned directly across from a Ferrari 330 P4. One head-turning car paired up with another extended for the length of the garage.

"I've only seen sketches of these. Where did you—?" he stopped, spinning around to stare at all the vehicles once more. He tried to speak again. "How did you—?"

Maddux gave up his attempt at completing a question. Obviously Rose had access to the latest prototypes in the auto industry and her team was capable of building them.

She stared up at him, a slight smile easing across her lips. "What were you expecting? Family sedans?"

"No, I just—I didn't realize you had access to these types of cars. This is like some fantasy land."

She laughed. "Well, maybe that's what you would call it. I call this my office."

"I never saw anything like this in New York."

"That's because we have different stipulations placed on us in the U.S. But in Europe, the sky is the limit. We can make these cars without fear of someone for *The New York Times* publishing a picture of one of these prototypes and sparking an inquiry into its origin. Some opportunistic photographer could compromise one of our agents by following the car and staking out the home of the driver. It'd be a nightmare."

"But in Europe?"

"No one cares. You see strange cars all over the place, not to mention people aren't generally obsessed with them in most of Europe like they are back home.

We've got half a dozen magazines that only write about cars, proving my point. Most guys think of their cars as an extension of themselves. It's quite silly, if you ask me."

"Yet here you are building these machines from the ground up."

"You're exactly right. The key word there is *machines*. Cars are little more than a complicated piece of equipment. A safe and reliable way to move someone from point A to point B. But if I didn't know any better, I would've thought cars were some special appendage that men have demonstrating their virility."

"There are men who think that way."

Rose huffed a short laugh through her nose. "If only all men could be as levelheaded as you."

"That's a grand assumption, isn't it?" he said, smiling.

"What's an assumption?"

"That I'm levelheaded and don't feel the same way about cars."

"Well, you don't, do you?"

Maddux let out a long slow breath. "Well, I—"

"You are, aren't you?" she said, interrupting. "You *are* just like them."

"For what it's worth, I usually only buy the kind of car that my employer sells. Now, if I could have any car in the world—"

"Stop right there," Rose said. "I don't want to know nor do I care. You don't have much time, and I need to show you the vehicle you need that will help you accomplish your mission."

"It wouldn't happen to be this Ferrari 330, would it?" he asked.

She cast a sideways glance at him. "There are some cars that will always draw too much attention, no matter where you drive them," she said. "And that's definitely one of them."

"So why even have it?"

"Focus, Ed," she said, wagging her index finger at him. "I need you to quit drooling over these cars and follow me." Rose walked to a corner of the garage where a car sat alone. "This is your automobile," she said, spreading her hands out wide.

"A Fiat Dino Spider," Maddux said, studying the car closely. "I've read about these. They're supposed to begin production in the next few months."

"I've been working on this one for several weeks," she said. "And I think you're going to like what you see."

Rose proceeded to give Maddux the run down of all the car's customized features that she added. However, the hidden smuggling compartment large enough to hold a person was the sole reason Maddux would be driving the Spider into Czechoslovakia. She stuck her head into the trunk and pointed out the special mirrors embedded into the sides and angled to increase the appearance of the trunk's size.

"That's how we create the illusion so inspectors think they are seeing the entire trunk," she said.

"I thought you only dealt in science, not magic," Maddux asked with a wry grin.

"Sometimes the two go hand in hand. But all you need to know is that you'll be able to breeze through any border inspections without raising an eyebrow."

"So you admit that magic is sometimes helpful?" he asked.

"It's possible that it could help you get out of a tight jam here and there."

"Do I need to show you my latest trick?"

She shook her head and glanced at her watch.

"You need to get back for your meeting with Pritchett. The last thing I want is to see him lumbering around my workspace, waving his hook in search of you."

"I could show you how to make him disappear when he starts acting like that."

"I'd rather you disappear upstairs to your meeting. Besides, don't you always say that *a good magician never reveals his tricks*?"

"Who said I was a good magician?"

"Get out of here," she said, gesturing toward the door. "I'll have the keys ready for you once you finish your meeting. Now, go."

Maddux exited Rose's hidden lair before returning upstairs for his meeting with Pritchett. Showing up two minutes late shouldn't have earned Maddux the reprimand that he received, but he could tell from the lines etched into Pritchett's forehead that he was in a foul mood.

"Sorry, I'm late," Maddux said. "Rose was showing me the car we'll be taking for this operation."

"No excuses, Maddux," Pritchett said, digging his hook into his desk. "We're all busy around here, not just you. My time is just as valuable, if not more so, than yours. Don't be late again."

"So, what's the plan?" Barbara asked.

In his rush to get to the meeting room, Maddux had barely recognized the meeting's other attendees.

Barbara Carson was seated to Maddux's right, while

a pair of State Department liaisons fanned out in chairs to his left.

Maddux leaned forward, anxious to hear the details of Pritchett's master plan. If there was one thing he'd learned in his short time since joining the agency, it was that details mattered. To pull off a successful operation, Maddux realized he needed to know as many details as possible and to possess the ability to translate that information into a workable plan if the original idea failed to produce results.

"It's a really simple mission," Pritchett said. "Barbara, you and Maddux drive to Prague, meet with your business contacts there, and then rendezvous with Voss and get him back across the border. Voss has a simple assignment, which is to place several bugs in strategic locations so our station there can do the rest. He's also going to try and get some pictures of the research facility there. But that's it. Nothing too complicated."

"And we're sure he's on board with the plan? Isn't there a possibility that he could sell us out?"

Pritchett shrugged. "There's always that possibility, Maddux. In the world of espionage, trust is never a given. However, you must take the leap from time to time in order to get what you want. You can live by a motto of *trust no one, question everything*, but that won't get you far. It'll just put you in a tinfoil hat while you live on the street somewhere, mumbling to yourself as strangers walk by."

"He seemed a little cagey, that's all."

"Well, it's your call out on the field. If you think you and Barbara are getting set up, feel free to bail. By that point, we'd have all the listening devices in place, so it wouldn't be a great loss. If Voss dared to tell on himself for planting the bugs, he'd be taking an incredibly great risk. Mikhailov would likely shoot him on the spot. Voss has plenty of reasons to return, including his wife and daughter, who are being closely watched in New York just in case he has other plans."

"Sounds simple enough," Maddux said. "What could go wrong?"

Barbara cut her eyes at Maddux and shook her head.

"You've got a lot to learn, rookie," she said as she stood.

Pritchett pushed a file across his desk to Maddux. "Read up on Voss and other alternate routes out of the country, just in case," Pritchett said. "You need to be more concerned about *when* something goes wrong, not *if*. You just never know how things are going to unfold when you get out beyond these walls and out on the field. Remember, the best laid plans—"

"Of mice and men often go awry. I know, I know."

Pritchett chuckled. "Actually, I was going to say the best laid plans are often never that great to begin with."

"You're not exactly instilling me with a lot of confidence with statements like that."

"Go give me a reason to be confident, Maddux. I know this is baptism by fire, but you're an important part of this mission. You're cleverly placed to pull this off before the StB even realizes what went wrong. You might remain on their radar for a week or two, but they'll be too proud to admit that you duped them. And that's why I know this mission has a great opportunity to succeed. Notice I didn't say plan."

"Are you trying to make me paranoid?"

"I can't make you into something that you already are. Now, go bring home Otto Voss and reunite him with his family. The poor man has been through enough as it is."

"Yes, sir," Maddux said as he stood.

"And take care of Barb for me, will you? She's practically family. I know she can hold her own, but don't let her get into a compromising situation, okay?"

Maddux nodded and tucked the file folder underneath his arm before exiting the room. He had plenty to think about during his walk back to his office at Opel, things far bigger than how to encourage people to buy his company's latest and greatest model car.

AFTER HIS FIRST DAY of meeting with Gregory
Mikhailov and other high-ranking StB officials to discuss
any intelligence gathered in the U.S., Otto Voss slipped
out of his hotel window, undetected by the agents who
were supposed to be watching him. Voss had picked up
on the fact that he was being followed and immediately
began to conjure up a plan to escape his hotel without
being detected.

While casually strolling downstairs to the hotel bar,
Voss slipped into the kitchen and meandered through
to the laundry room. Once there, he handed a woman a
ten-dollar bill in exchange for one of the hotel's uni-
forms worn by the servers. Voss wasted no time in leaving through the back to find a pay phone.

He walked for several blocks, constantly glancing
over his shoulder to see if he was being followed. When
he grew suspicious, he'd ease into an alleyway after
rounding a corner and hide behind any object he could
find that was large enough to conceal him in the darkness. Once Voss was convinced he'd adverted danger,

he would re-emerge and continue his search for a pay phone.

Between the growing paranoia and navigating the streets beneath the dimly lit overhead lamps, Voss finally found what he was looking for. He dropped five korunas into the slot and dialed Ingrid's number. An operator instructed him to deposit an extra *pF tka* before continuing. He complied, tapping nervously on the receiver as he waited for her to answer.

"Hello?" she said.

"Ingrid?" Voss said.

"Otto! Where are you now? I've been worried sick about you. Poor Astrid, too. We're both a mess. Please tell me you're coming home soon."

"Yes, very soon," he said.

"Where are you?"

"I had to come back to Prague and take care of a little business," he said as he glanced around at the empty street. He watched intently as a man strode by along the sidewalk. Voss fixed his eyes on a nearby puddle, perfectly reflecting the man's face as he passed. To Voss, the man looked like a normal businessman returning home from a long day of work. Voss slowly turned his head to follow the man. By the time Voss craned his neck to see almost entirely behind his current position, the man was gone.

"Otto! Otto! Otto, are you listening?" Ingrid demanded.

"Oh, yes, dear. I was listening to everything you said."

"Everything?" she asked.

"Yes, I heard every word of it."

"Well, what was the last thing I asked you?"

Voss paused for a moment before launching into a story about how she asked him if he was sure he was supposed to be doing this. Then he proceeded to compose a long-winded response about how it was his civic duty to stop evil. She stopped him long before he could finish.

"Listen to me," she said. "I asked you if you wanted to speak with Astrid because she misses you terribly, as do I."

"Oh, yes, of course, I do. Please, put her on."

"Forget it," Ingrid said. "Just be careful, and come home soon."

She hung up, the click resounding in Voss's ears.

He tried not to take offense at her anger as he attempted to be sympathetic toward the situation he'd placed her in. After all, he had left her without any warning to fly halfway around the world without giving her a reason.

She'll come around.

He hung up his receiver and stepped lightly into the puddle near the pay phone, the face of the man who'd passed by still burned into memory. Voss wondered if he was being watched despite the absence of any visible pedestrians along the street.

He kept his head down as he hustled back to the hotel. Once he reached the alleyway door, he opened it then removed the rock he'd placed to ensure he had access to the building. After quickly changing, he wound his way back to the main reception area and walked upstairs. He noticed the men who'd been there before watching him closely were gone.

When Voss inserted his key into the door of his hotel room, the door pushed open, already ajar. Pressing lightly against it, a high-pitched creak emanated from the hinges.

"*Ahoj*?" he asked as he entered his room. "Hello?"

There was no response.

When the door fully opened, Voss stared agape at the room. All of his clothes and other belongings were strewn about. The chair cushions were scattered on the floor. The bed sat off kilter. In the bathroom, every towel that had been stacked so neatly for him laid in a pile at the foot of the toilet.

Voss jingled the coins in his pocket, grateful that he'd made the decision not to store the intelligence in his luggage. Keeping the secrets in his pocket likely helped him avoid a late-night meeting with Mikhailov. Voss had endured one of those before—but just barely. He didn't want to experience the wrath of Mikhailov again.

Convinced that the StB agents assigned to watch him were simply awaiting a chance to look through his belongings, Voss left the hotel again. This time, he didn't look over his shoulder. He marched six blocks to his former home, clenching his fists as he went. Along the way as he passed each person on the sidewalk, Voss tensed up expecting a fight. But each person passed by without as much as a glance.

Voss walked into the lobby only to find that the elevator was still inoperable. For once, he wished he didn't have to climb a dozen flights of stairs. He was tired of all the extra time to think, preferring to take action as soon as possible.

When he entered the floor, he turned and noticed

his apartment door wide open. He poked his head inside to find the entire place trashed. What furniture remained had been destroyed, likely by vandals or teenagers just having a little fun. Some of the clothes remained, though most of it was soiled or covered in dust.

Stepping on what sounded like a broken piece of glass, Voss scooted to the side and stooped down to see what crunched beneath his feet. He carefully picked up a picture frame, the glass splintering from the upper left corner. Forcing a smile, he lingered on the photo for a moment, one that had been taken on his wedding day.

Ingrid looked so beautiful.

Just the thought stirred up his regret again. Voss questioned if his lust for revenge had gone too far. He could've passed intel—the kind that mixed faulty with meaningless—to Mikhailov for years and avoided any kind of threats of retribution. But Voss knew he couldn't do that forever. And it would've only been a matter of time before Mikhailov made more serious threats and wouldn't have thought twice about exposing Voss if a more reliable source came along. And Voss knew it. His mission of revenge was as much about survival as it was about retaliation.

The scene spread out before Voss only fueled his fire. He swore he'd get his revenge, regardless of whether or not the Americans wanted to go along with him or not. One way or another, he'd be free very soon.

BONN, GERMANY

MADDUX AROSE THE NEXT MORNING, carrying on the ruse that the day was just another normal one in his workweek. But instead of files in his brief case, he'd packed some clothes. There would be more for him stashed inside the car he would drive with Barbara, but he remained particular about the type of boxers he wore. He doubted the government-issued variety would meet his stringent standards.

He locked the door to his apartment, sure to snag an extra key for his body double, who would leave the Opel offices around 5:30 p.m. and pretend to be Maddux for several days. The agent would keep Maddux's schedule while keeping his head down to avoid drawing any suspicion. While Pritchett often complained in meeting about using trained agents in this manner, such was the game. Maddux was all too aware that Pritchett might endanger the cover of his civilian assets in certain situations if there were no other viable options.

Once Maddux exited through the bowels of the building and entered the CIA station, he immediately reported downstairs, where Rose awaited him. Maddux sported a navy suit and tie along with a grey fedora.

Rose greeted him at the door with a smile. "You're looking a little extra snazzy today," Rose said as she walked up to him and straightened his tie. "If I didn't know any better, I would've thought you got all dressed up for me."

Maddux grinned and was about to say something when the sound of a woman clearing her throat in the corner of the room made them both pause and look in her direction.

"We need to get on the road as soon as possible," Barbara Carson said. "Please save the flirtatious banter for a day when we have more time. We must get moving."

Rose sighed and released Maddux's tie.

"This wasn't flirting," Rose said, holding up a tie clip. "I was putting this clever device on your partner here. It just might save your life."

"What does it do?" Maddux asked.

She flipped the clip over and squeezed its sides, producing a sharp blade. "It's not much, but when you're in a bind during a fight, it could make all the difference."

Rose forced a smile and nodded emphatically at Barbara.

"Don't expect an apology from me, honey," Barbara said. "That clip is only a nice little cover for you."

Maddux stepped back. "Will you knock it off, Barb? Rose is just doing her job here."

Barbara held her steely gaze on Rose. "I guess I didn't get the memo about the new perks the Office of Technical Services personnel will now be providing."

Rose draped a gold chain over her hand and held it up toward Barbara. "I have an exploding locket for you, if you're interested," Rose said. "The perks here are for everyone."

Barbara trudged across the room toward Rose and took the piece of jewelry in her hand.

"If you open up the locket and depress this button, you have three seconds to throw it before it explodes," Rose said. "I would give you a demonstration, but it's a one-time use only device."

Barbara fastened the necklace around her neck. "I'll figure it out."

"Well, since we've settled that, let me show you some of the other objects I think will be of benefit for your mission," Rose said, motioning for them to join her as she walked toward a long row of tables.

"It's a pretty simple mission," Barbara said.

"Yes, but one that could be fraught with danger," Rose said. "I read a brief of the operation and discussed it with Pritchett. He approved all of these devices, agreeing with me that they could all come in useful if you find yourself in a pinch."

"Let's see 'em," Maddux said, rubbing his hands together.

Rose picked up a pair of men's shoes off the table. "If you knock the heels of this shoe hard, a blade slides out of the front like this," she said as she demonstrated. "You just never know when you're going to need that extra oomph."

"You're really into blades," Maddux said.

Rose nodded. "Guns are out of play in hand-to-hand combat, not to mention they're difficult to hide.

But knives seem to be handy and easily concealable."

Barbara sighed. "So, is this so Maddux here can play the hero and save the day? I'm sure there's nothing in my shoes."

"Actually, there is," Rose said, picking up a pair of women's shoes. "I rigged this pair to emit a smoke screen by tapping the toe on the ground forcefully."

Barbara shrugged. "Could be useful."

Rose drifted away from the table and moved toward the vehicles. "Now, this is the most important tool for your mission—the Fiat Dino Spider."

Maddux ran his hand along the car's contours and whistled.

"I've already shown Maddux how the special compartment works," Rose said to Barbara while opening the trunk. "That's where you'll store your asset for the ride back into Germany. It's far more comfortable than it looks." Rose completed her demonstration of how it worked before slamming the trunk closed. "Any questions?"

"I'm good," Maddux said before turning to Barbara. "And you?"

"We should be fine."

"Excellent," Rose said. "If you run into any problems, you know how to reach me." She handed the keys to Maddux. "Try not to fall in love," Rose said with a wink.

"I may not give her back," he said as he strode around to the passenger door and opened it. He gestured for Barbara to get in.

"What makes you think you're driving?" Barbara said, refusing to budge.

"Oh, come on, Barbara. Really?"

"Fine," she said. "I'll let you drive for the first half of the trip. But I will take over. Border guards have a weakness for women drivers."

Maddux waited until she was seated before closing the door and walking around to the driver's side. He glanced at Rose, who was staring mindlessly at the ground.

"Thanks, Rose," he said, snapping her out of her daze.

"I know all these things are going to be most helpful."

"I hope you don't have to use them," she said, fiddling with her golden necklace.

"That's not going to explode, is it?" Maddux said, nodding toward her chain.

"Oh, no," she said with a chuckle before turning serious. "At least, I hope not. Now, get outta here. Go bring back that scientist."

Maddux climbed into the car and twisted the key in the ignition. The engine roared to life while a door at the far end of the garage slid open. He eased onto the gas and exited Rose's hidden lair. They traveled up several floors of a parking garage until they reached the street level. He pulled onto the road, and they began their journey to Prague.

* * *

NEITHER MADDUX NOR BARBARA spoke for the first half hour of their trip. With arms crossed and a constant scowl worn on her face, Barbara didn't appear to be in the mood to talk. But Maddux decided that the uncomfortable silence was worse than prying into the reason behind Barbara's bad mood, though he had a good idea of the cause.

"Are you always this chatty?" Maddux asked.

Barbara cast a sideways glance at him and tapped her foot rhythmically on the floorboard.

He took a different tact. "I mean, if there's something you want to talk about . . ."

"I really don't need a shrink, Maddux," she said, eyes remaining focused on the road in front of them.

"Well, this is long trip, and I just thought—"

"See, right there, that's your problem. You're thinking."

"I'm trying to be friendly."

She shook her head, huffing a laugh through her nose.

"What?" he asked.

"You're unlike any spy I've ever met," she said.

"What do you mean?"

"You're just too damn polite. You're worried about my feelings. You don't want this car ride to be an uncomfortable one. You're the antithesis of me."

"I take it that bothers you," Maddux said.

"It annoys the hell out of me, to be honest. I just want to do my job and go home every night. I don't want to be psychoanalyzed by some agent who is still wet behind the ears. Is that too much to ask?"

"You could ask for worse, I guess."

"Look, we have to work together. I get it. But I don't have to like it."

Maddux drove on in silence for another ten minutes before reigniting their conversation. "Who did you work with before?"

"Tim Felton, God rest his soul."

"Killed on an operation with you?"

"You could say that."

"What happened?"

"I put a bullet in his head."

Maddux's eyes widened, and he clutched the steering wheel so hard that the color began to fade from his knuckles.

"Don't worry, Maddux. I only shoot traitors."

"What did he do?"

"I caught him sleeping with a known KGB operative," she said. "Felton claimed it was his way of getting secrets out of her, but I knew better. We'd had several ops fail in the previous month, and I started to suspect that someone was leaking information to the KGB. When I suggested to him that maybe someone was passing intel to the enemy, he quickly dismissed the idea, insisting that no one would betray their country like that. That's when I started to wonder if he was the one."

"And you caught him?"

"Sort of. He had a cache of secret documents sitting out on the coffee table when I walked into his apartment one day. He was wearing a towel when he came to the door and said he was about to take a shower. I pushed my way past him and ran back to his bedroom where I found the KGB agent wrapped in his sheets. Since I wasn't carrying a weapon, I immediately went for hers on the nightstand and snatched the gun just before she could grab it. I knocked her out with the butt of the gun and then shot her in the side of the head at point blank range."

"And where was Felton?"

"He was cowering in the corner, crying. He was begging me not to tell our station chief, so I agreed—and then shot him. The Bonn police called it a murder-suicide and reported to the press that it was the kind of story made for a tragic spy novel. Two agents from different countries fall in love. One wants to leave their vocations behind and escape their lives. But then the woman finds out that she was spurned and that the man has a family back home. He told her he never had any intention of leaving his family for her. So, she ends his life and then her own. Classic tragic love story. The press ran the story on the front pages of German newspapers here. Meanwhile, I kept my word about Felton. You're the only person who knows the full story now."

Maddux kept his eyes on the road and remained quiet, trying to digest all he'd just heard.

"Sorry you asked, aren't you?" she said.

Maddux shook his head. "That's not it at all."

Another long moment of silence.

"You loved him, didn't you?" Maddux asked.

"What?"

"You were lovers, weren't you?"

"What makes you think that?"

"You're not answering my question."

She sighed. "Guilty as charged."

"So, did you shoot him out of loyalty to your country or in a jealous rage?"

"I'm sure there was a little of both involved."

"Fair enough," Maddux said. "I wouldn't doubt you if you claimed your reasoning was a hundred percent either way."

"Love is a cruel mistress in this profession. She

taunts you with something you can't really have and then teases you with a poor imitation. Because love in this business is never really love—it's about escaping for just a few minutes from a lifetime of loneliness."

"What does your family think you do?" Maddux asked.

"They think I'm a secretary hunting for some rich European man."

"I'm sure you find such opinions irritating."

Barbara laughed. "Irritating? No, that's what you call the radio signal flickering in and out during the chorus to your favorite song. Infuriating is what it's like to have your family think you're just some lackey for a company big shot."

"So, how do you handle lying to them?"

"It's painful," she said. "I'm not going to lie about that. I hate doing it. But I do it because I know that my work at the agency matters. The information we gather, the missions we undertake, the danger we put ourselves in—all of those things help keep our country safe. And even more importantly to me, those things keep my family safe. I know they'd never understand, even if I told them. But I got over that a long time ago. Sometimes the most important things we do don't have explanations that are easily understood by others. But we must all follow that call, that sense of duty we possess."

"Your decision to join the agency looks like it has cost you something you strongly desire."

"What's that?"

"Love."

She chuckled and shook her head. "My greatest fear is dying alone. And perhaps love is the only way to mitigate that, but it's simply a means to an end in my book."

"That's not exactly my idea of love, but I understand where you're coming from."

"Good," she said. "I'd prefer not to work with a partner who is looking down on me with some sort of moral superiority."

Maddux checked his mirrors and continued along the highway before Barbara eventually broke the silence.

"If you're thinking about falling in love, don't. That's the advice I'd give any agent—even though I know you weren't directly asking."

"But I—"

"Save it, Maddux," she said. "I saw the way you looked at Rose."

"What do you mean? I was just—"

"Don't even try to fool me, even though you might be trying to fool yourself. I know that you two worked together on a case in New York. There's something going on there, I know. But just for your own sake—and for hers—don't go there."

Maddux decided that defending himself would only make him look more desperate in Barbara's eyes. If he were pressed to answer if he liked Rose or not, he wasn't sure how he'd respond. However, based on Barbara's comments, his affinity for Rose must've been glaringly obvious. And if Barbara could tell how he felt, Rose probably could too.

The thought irked Maddux. He gripped the steering wheel tightly again and eased onto the gas pedal as they sped toward Prague.

THEY PULLED INTO PRAGUE just before 6:00 p.m. and headed directly to the manufacturing plant for their meeting with Barum Auto. Once they passed through the guard gate, Barum CEO Anton Dvorak stood waiting for them at the front entrance.

Using his briefcase to shield himself from the guard dogs, Maddux could barely hear Dvorak over the barking. Three of the dogs circled around the car as if they were preparing to attack their prey.

"*Drž hubu*," Dvorak shouted.

The dogs quickly quieted down, hustling to his side.

Maddux and Barbara walked in Dvorak's direction.

"Please accept my apologies," Dvorak said. "My girls can get a little overprotective sometimes. Come with me."

Dvorak gestured for the dogs to leave, and they obeyed immediately, hustling back around the corner of the building. Dvorak then led them inside Barum's facilities.

"I trust you are not too tired from you drive," he

said. "We could postpone until the morning if you don't feel up to meeting now."

"It wasn't that difficult of a drive," Maddux said.

"I've heard those Fiats are comfortable automobiles," Dvorak said. "But I am curious why you didn't travel here in one of your own vehicles. That doesn't exactly give me confidence in our potential partnership."

Maddux laughed. "I agreed to bring this car here for a friend, a friend who doesn't work with us at Opel. But trust me, I wouldn't be driving a Fiat unless I absolutely had to, though I will add that car is faster than anything we produce currently in Germany. However, we're not looking to enter into the fast car market, are we? We're looking to manufacture dependable automobiles for the everyday person."

"Let me give you a tour around so you can see our plant," Dvorak said.

The Czech businessman spoke proudly and confidently about his company and the people who worked for him. Most of the employees had gone home for the evening, but there were still a few operating some of the more specialized lines, detailing cars and adding non-standard packages. Dvorak strode along the platform on the second floor that created a perimeter overlooking the bulk of the manufacturing activity below. He paused occasionally to point out some of their innovations unique to their automobiles.

For the most part, the plant seemed like a normal operation. But the presence of several armed guards created some concern for Maddux. He watched as the men roamed around, stopping only to bark out orders to a fellow guard below on the main floor. As Dvorak led

Maddux and Barbara downstairs again, Maddux paused by the window and took note of the additional security around the perimeter. Barbed wire topped the twelve-foot-high fence encircling the property, while a sentry tower was positioned on the far corner, overlooking the grounds.

Once Dvorak completed the tour, he led them back to his office and invited them to sit down.

"What do you think of our operation?" Dvorak asked as a wide grin spread across his face.

"Impressive," Barbara said. "You seem to have quite the operation here."

"And you, Mr. Maddux? What did you think?"

"I agree with Barbara," Maddux said. "This place seems to ooze with excellence."

"So you think we could meet Opel's strict standards?" Dvorak asked.

"Absolutely," Maddux said. "Maybe even Opel could learn a thing or two from you as well."

Dvorak's eyes lit up. "Really? What do you think we do better than Opel?"

"Security," Maddux said. "I don't believe I've ever seen a plant so tightly secured in all my life."

"Thank you, Mr. Maddux. That means a lot to me as I've taken it upon myself to oversee that side of our business. Our security team is still a work in progress, but we've managed to deter more thieves than not who've come here in hopes of making off with a significant bounty."

"What is it exactly that these thieves are after?" Barbara asked.

"Scrap metal," Dvorak said. "That commodity is

worth quite a bit of korunas on the open market—and very hard to come by these days. Even though the war ended about two decades ago, the rebuilding effort has just now hit our country in recent years, and demand for all things metal is incredibly high. If we didn't have such good suppliers from other countries with prices already locked in, I'm not sure we would be able to build an affordable automobile."

"Interesting," Maddux said. "I never considered such challenges a country like yours might face."

Dvorak clasped his hands together and leaned forward on his desk. "Let's pause with the history lesson for a moment and get down to business," he said. "I really want to discuss how you plan to support us in a mutually beneficial partnership when it comes to marketing our cars."

Maddux opened his briefcase and pulled out a dossier that he handed to Dvorak. "I think this should give you a good idea of what we're thinking and where we're headed."

* * *

AFTER THE MEETING, Maddux and Barbara checked into their hotel and enjoyed a brief dinner. Over a couple glasses of wine, they discussed the most troubling aspect of their meeting with Dvorak—the large number of armed guards roaming around Barum's property.

"It doesn't make sense," Maddux said.

"What?" Barbara asked.

"His explanation about scrap metal."

"I've heard similar stories from other nations that are struggling under the oppressive thumb of the Russians."

"I don't know how much stock I put in that. It just seemed like overkill."

"Unless perhaps the thieves Dvorak referenced are coming with tanks."

Maddux chuckled at Barbara's witty comment.

"The guards looked like they were prepared for a gunfight with someone," he said.

"I doubt they would win though."

"Did you see some weaknesses?"

"They didn't appear to be trained," she said. "Guards who've undergone proper training wouldn't be so visible. The most effective types of guards are the ones who blend into the background and only make themselves known if necessary. Those guys might as well have hung placards around their necks and carried megaphones to announce their presence."

"Good point. My hunch is they are hiding something else there. I know we're really here for other reasons, but sometimes fortune favors the bold."

"I'm not sure I would call what we did *bold*. It was just a business meeting—a legitimate business meeting, by the way."

Maddux leaned in close, speaking in a whisper. "Going unarmed behind enemy lines qualifies as bold in my book. If they'd known who we were, Dvorak could've gutted us right there and there wouldn't have been a thing we could've done about it."

"You could've fought back with that tie clip of yours," Barbara said with a wink.

Maddux glanced down at his chest and inspected the device. "Can't fault Rose for trying," he said. "I didn't need it today, but you never know."

"If I were a man, I'd just remove my tie and use it to choke my opponent to death."

Maddux's eyes widened. "The more I get to know you, the more frightened I am of your violent side."

"My violent side doesn't come out very often, only when it's forced into service or I need it to defend myself."

"I'll keep that in mind," Maddux said.

"So, are you ready to retire for the evening?" she asked.

"I'm done if you are."

"Excellent," she said. "I need to get some rest—or not."

She gave him an alluring look.

"Let me walk you to your room and get you to bed," Maddux said.

She glared at him. "Do I look drunk to you?"

Maddux shook his head. "Just want to make sure you're all right."

"In case you've forgotten, I need to stay sharp tonight for when we get the call."

Maddux held his hand up, hoping to prevent Barbara from divulging any more information in case prying ears were listening. "Let's go."

He led her down the hallway and to her room. At her door, Barbara fumbled through her purse. After a short search, she hoisted her key in the air and winked. "Found it."

Maddux ushered her inside and shut the door behind him.

"You think I'm that easy, Maddux," she said as she sat on the bed and began taking off her shoes.

"No, no," Maddux said. "I just wanted to—"

"You just wanted to what? Dip your toe in the waters?"

"Barbara, I'm a gentleman. I don't know what you're trying to do here, but despite your good looks, I'm going to stay focused on the job at hand. We're expecting a call from the asset at ten o'clock. Once we hear from him, I'll affirm our plan to meet in the morning to get him out of the country."

"I know all that," she said, waving at him dismissively. "That means we've got fifteen minutes to kill."

Maddux didn't flinch. "Why don't you read a book? In the meantime, I'm going back to my room and will wait for his call. I'll knock on your door when I hear from him and update you on the plan. Sound good?"

"I guess."

She sighed and reclined on the bed, gazing distantly at a painting of wildflowers on the wall.

"I never pegged you to be such a bore," she added.

"Sorry to disappoint you," Maddux said. "Besides, I'm on duty right now."

"There's no law against having a little fun while you're on the clock."

"Perhaps we don't share the same ideas about what constitutes *fun*."

She rolled her eyes. "I also never would've pegged you for a prude, Maddux."

"I'll take your new assessment as a compliment."

He quickly exited and headed down the hall for his room. Hearing her mumble something as he shut the door, he didn't care to go back and get clarification. Besides, he knew any romantic interlude with Barbara would be a waste of time, not that he was in search of one. He just knew they'd never work out. Her sharp tongue and brash manner wasn't one he found attractive.

He sat at the foot of his bed and got undressed. With just his t-shirt and boxers still on, he donned a soft robe and fuzzy slippers—and hoped no one would ever see him like that. He realized he'd have to get dressed again once Voss called, but Maddux didn't care. He needed a few minutes to sit down and relax.

Glancing at the clock, he noticed the appointed time to hear from Voss was drawing near. At 10:00 p.m., Maddux sat on the edge of his bed and stared at the phone, waiting for it to ring.

"If a watched pot never boils, does a watched phone never ring?" he wondered aloud.

The minutes ticked past. Five minutes then ten and fifteen.

At 10:30 p.m., Maddux still sat watching the phone, contemplating the idea that perhaps there was a miscommunication somewhere. He dug out a piece of paper that had all the details inscribed on it.

Nope. He was supposed to call at 10:00 p.m.

Still nothing.

Maddux was officially concerned.

XIII

OTTO VOSS PICKED UP a copy of *Lidové Noviny* on his way to his meeting with Gregory Mikhailov and several other StB officials. The date jumped off the page at Voss. He took a deep breath and tucked the newspaper underneath his arm. Scanning the rest of the pedestrians crowded around the street corner waiting to cross the street, he spotted one StB agent. There were probably more, but he couldn't readily identify any.

The light changed, and the throng of people moved like a swarm of insects across the street. He glanced around to see if he was still being watched—and he was.

Moving mindlessly along the sidewalk, Voss reached into his pocket and felt the pair of listening devices he was to plant at the request of the CIA's station chief. If he didn't go along with the American's plan, Voss would likely end up in a tragic accident before he attempted to leave the country, never to be seen again. If he sought refuge with the StB, he would likely be tortured and would never see Ingrid and Astrid again. But if he succeeded . . .

Voss didn't really have a choice, though he wasn't

sure he wanted one. The only chance he had to escape the virtual prison to which he'd been confined was to execute the plan and hope the CIA kept its word. But even that option meant he'd spend the rest of his life looking over his shoulder, praying Mikhailov wouldn't be coming. Voss decided that was no way to live. In light of what he'd learned about his tormentor, Voss had a new plan so he wouldn't have to live in constant fear— kill Mikhailov and then disappear forever.

Voss tapped his breast pocket, the hiding place he selected for the secret camera he also received from the CIA. The wire sewn into his jacket stretched the length of his left sleeve and a few inches beyond, just enough for him to click the small attached device to capture photos. The camera was sewn into his jacket button and would be difficult to detect for even the best-trained eye. Voss had stared at it for more than half an hour in an attempt to see how the device was wired. Eventually, he gave up, resigning himself to the fact that he didn't need to know how it worked, just that it did.

After fifteen minutes of casual walking, Voss arrived at the front doors of the StB offices. While the presence of their agents was supposed to remain a secret, the location of their offices wasn't. Everyone in Prague knew exactly how to reach the country's secret police. If anything, the transparency of their site gave citizens an avenue to alert the agency to any suspicious happenings. As a result, reporting neighbors to the StB had also become a way of retaliation for wayward behavior. While such tattling had to be utilized judiciously, it remained an effective revenge tool.

Voss peeled off from the crowd, noticing how odd it

seemed for the horde of people to continue moving along without anyone else taking a detour into the StB headquarters. He stood in the lobby for nearly two minutes and didn't see another person enter or exit the building.

"May I help you?" the man asked.

"I'm here to meet Gregory Mikhailov," Voss said.

The security guard nodded toward the receptionist and then mouthed "Gregory Mikhailov." The woman nodded, picked up her phone, and dialed a number.

"He'll be with you shortly," the guard said. He gestured toward a handful of chairs in the corner. "You can have a seat in our waiting area over there."

"Thank you," Voss said before taking a seat.

He dug into his pocket and felt the pair of listening devices. Carefully taking them out one at a time, he tucked them in his shirt collar. If guards chose to search him, they would find nothing, though Voss doubted he would ever be searched. Mikhailov would consider such an act an exercise in paranoia. He was far too confident and proud to even admit that someone would dare attempt a double-cross.

After a minute, Mikhailov sauntered down the steps, flanked by a pair of guards.

"Search him," Mikhailov said.

Voss's jaw dropped as he stood. Disbelief settled over his face before he could muster up the strength to speak.

"You look like you've seen a ghost," Mikhailov said with a straight face.

Voss didn't move as guards patted him down.

When they finished, Mikhailov threw his arms around Voss.

"Welcome back," Mikhailov said. "I wasn't sure if you'd return for another day of debriefing or if you were going to steal away into the night like you did before."

Voss let out a long slow breath and began walking with Mikhailov.

"That was a long time ago," Voss said. "Let's focus on the present, shall we?"

"But of course."

They walked upstairs to Mikhailov's office in silence before sitting down. Mikhailov leaned back in his chair, interlocking his fingers behind his head.

"We had a chance to inspect your intelligence," he said in a matter-of-fact tone.

"I trust you found it to be good," Voss said.

Mikhailov shrugged. "It was—how should I say it—mediocre at best."

"What do you mean?"

"We knew most of the information that you gave us with the exception of a few pieces. However, none of it was the kind of intel we really wanted."

"The Americans expect me to divulge everything, but they are keeping me in the dark about their plans," Voss said, leaning forward in his chair.

"I seriously doubt that's true. You see, I know you happen to possess the knowledge they need. And if you refused to give it to them after all this time, they surely would've dispensed with you by now."

"I swear, Gregory, on my mother's grave that I know nothing more than what I've told you."

Mikhailov shook his head, rested his arms on his chair, and clucked his tongue. "You know, Otto, I thought you had more integrity than that. But to sell out your own mother so quickly. And for what? Just to try and fool me into believing your outright lies."

Voss narrowed his eyes. "I don't know why you have such a hard time believing what I'm saying, but I swear to you that it's true. The Americans don't flaunt their plans in front of everyone. It took me months just to get the information that I brought back."

Mikhailov slammed his fist on his desk and leaned forward. "Then I expect better than this," he said before slinging the quarter containing the microdot across the room. "Your intelligence was rubbish."

"I can only give you what they give me," Voss argued. He leaned back in his chair and stared at the floor. After a sigh, he considered continuing but thought better of it.

"I need to have a word with one of my officers," Mikhailov said before standing abruptly and exiting his office. He slammed his door shut so hard that it rattled for a few seconds.

As Mikhailov stomped down the hall, Voss wasted no time in springing into action, inserting one of the bugs inside Mikhailov's phone and placing the other in a small slot beneath his chair. After finishing, Voss exhaled and leaned back in his seat.

Less than a minute later, Mikhailov stormed back into the room. He shut the door and locked it before turning to Voss.

"I just had a word with one of my men," Mikhailov began. "It seems like you've been playing us for fools for quite some time."

Voss scowled. "What are you talking about? Why would I do anything for the Americans after they rejected me the way they did?"

"Revenge? Personal vendetta? I can't be privy to everyone's reasoning for why they do what they do. All I know is that you have broken the trust of this office and will be dealt with summarily."

"That makes no sense. The Americans are the one that rejected me. *You* are the only one who gave me a second chance. Why would I express any disloyalty toward you?"

"I am no fool," Mikhailov said with a growl. "You are going to pay a steep price for your indiscretions."

"Tell me what I've done then. At the very least, you owe me that, especially to a man who risked everything to bring you this information."

Mikhailov's phone rang. He stared at it for a moment and let it ring three times before finally answering. "What?"

Voss strained to hear but couldn't make out any of the other caller's words.

"I'll be right down," Mikhailov said before hanging up.

He stood and pointed at Voss. "You stay right here. I'll be back to deal with you. I must handle this emergency first."

Voss waited until Mikhailov was gone before venturing into the hallway. Checking to see if he was gone, Voss scurried back inside the office and started taking photos. He pulled out a stack of files and snapped picture after picture with the secret camera hidden in his jacket. Without much consideration given to the information he was looking at, Voss figured he must have clicked the button hidden inside his sleeve at least fifty times before he heard footfalls approaching.

Voss shoved the files in the top desk drawer and sat back in his chair. The officer continued down the hall without even glancing into Mikhailov's office. After waiting until the hallway was quiet, Voss stood and started searching for a way out of the office without getting caught. He realized he was in danger and needed a quick exit plan.

He opened the window and poked his head out. The leap down was a long one and would've been on the street right in front of a mindless crowd of people moving along the sidewalk. If he didn't break his leg in the drop, Voss figured someone would likely follow the suspicious activity and report it to the StB in hopes of attaining a handsome reward.

Voss decided his next best option was to make a break for it, albeit a stealthy one. He eyed a janitorial cart sitting dormant in the hallway and started to push it. Snatching a hat from the coat rack of a commanding officer, Voss tugged it low across his face and pushed the cart forward. He made it to the elevator and was inside before a pair of guards stormed inside and grabbed him.

"What are you doing?" Voss asked. "I need to clean the restroom on the first floor."

"Otto Voss, you aren't fooling anyone," one of the guards said as he squeezed Voss's arm. "You're coming with us."

"I'm afraid there's been a huge mistake," Voss said.

"No," the guard said, tightening his grip, "there hasn't."

Voss reluctantly marched forward, prodded by the pair of men behind him. They continued on until they reached the stairwell. The men shoved Voss, pushing him down several flights until they reached the bottom.

Voss stood at the doorway, unwilling to tug on the handle.

"If you don't open it, I'll crack your skull open," the guard said before breaking into a maniacal laugh.

Voss pulled gently on the door, which gave way easily and opened into a dark corridor. He didn't budge.

One of the guards put his foot into Voss's back and shoved him.

"You need to move," the man said.

Voss stumbled forward for several meters before standing upright. He looked to his left and right, identifying cell doors designed to entrap prisoners. Forlorn men appeared in the small openings covered only by iron bars. They muttered things to Voss as he moved forward at the prodding of the guards.

"Let them shoot you," one man said. "It'll be better than the hell you're about to endure."

"A bullet in the back is better than a minute in the cell," another man said.

With a swift shove from a guard's foot, Voss sprawled face first into the ground. He remained on the floor for a moment, unsure if he even wanted to attempt to get back on his feet.

"That's right," one of the prisoners yelled. "Just lay there. Make them do the work."

Voss pushed himself up, scrambling to his knees. He gritted his teeth and tried to stand. The moment he became fully upright, one of the guards shoved.

"Don't give in," another prisoner screamed. "Make them shoot you first."

Voss didn't have a chance to do anything other than

move forward before his head was slammed into the wall. A door to his left swung open, and Voss was forced through it.

"What are you doing this for?" Voss asked. "I've done nothing wrong."

The guards worked quickly to affix Voss's hands to a hook hanging from the ceiling in the middle of the cell. One of the men cranked a shaft, yanking Voss's hands upward until he hung several inches off the floor.

"Director Mikhailov will be here shortly," one of the men said before the two guards exited the room.

Voss hung there for at least an hour and felt all the blood drain from his arms. Even if he were released immediately, he'd need five minutes to feel normal again. He tingled throughout his upper body and prayed that he'd soon be rid of the pain coursing through him.

The door eventually swung open and Mikhailov walked through, snapping a cropping stick.

"It's time we had a talk, Otto," Mikhailov said. "A real talk."

Two men untied Voss and lowered him to the floor. Voss wobbled as he tried to stand upright.

Mikhailov grinned before he unleashed his fury on Voss.

The first blow knocked Voss off balance. The next, a swift kick to his knees, knocked him to the ground. Mikhailov put his knee into Voss's chest before delivering a combination of punches. Jabs, haymakers, upper-cuts. In less than two minutes, Voss's eyes were so swollen he could barely see his tormentor looming over him.

"That's enough," another man boomed, leading to a

halt in the assault.

Voss tried to make out the face of the man who commanded enough power to make Mikhailov stop. But the combination of distance and darkness kept the man's identity anonymous.

"Clean him up," the man said. "We're not done with him yet."

Voss didn't move. If Mikhailov wanted to put Voss somewhere else, he determined the monster was going to have to use sheer strength.

I won't take one step for that bastard.

Voss watched his defiance get rewarded as the pair of guards lifted him off the prison cell floor and dragged him across the room and into the hallway.

"I thought you learned your lesson," Mikhailov chided. "But, apparently, I was wrong about you. I suppose I'll have to resort to some other methods of extracting information out of you now."

"I don't understand," Voss said. "What have I done? I've been nothing but loyal to you."

Mikhailov sprinted down the hallway and leaned over, speaking directly into Voss's right ear. "You want to talk about loyalty? Let's talk about loyalty. Let's talk about the time you tried to escape the country—or the multiple times you refused to assist in this operation."

"And then you had to resort to cheap parlor tricks to force me to join you."

Mikhailov stopped and the guards along with him. He moved directly in front of Voss and stooped down to get eye to eye with him. "Cheap parlor tricks? Whatever on earth are you talking about?"

Blood oozed from the corner of Voss's mouth. He

turned to his right, wiping his mouth on his sleeve. "I think you know exactly what I'm talking about."

Mikhailov smirked. "If I do, then you don't have much of a defense, do you? I know that you've been talking to the Americans—and they've been brainwashing you."

"Brainwashing is your specialty."

Mikhailov smiled and shook his head. "Hardly my forte. But you're about to find out firsthand what it is."

Mikhailov looked at the guards and snapped before pointing down the hallway. The men nodded knowingly and resumed lugging Voss.

"You bastard," Voss yelled. "You ruined my family."

"And now I'm going to ruin your life for good."

Voss tensed, rage coursing through his veins. He just wanted to take one free shot at the StB official. Due to all the pent-up anger, Voss was convinced he could kill Mikhailov with just one punch. It was only a theory, but Voss was itching to test it out.

He just needed to live long enough to experiment.

XIV

AT 10:30 P.M., MADDUX WAS concerned about Voss. By 11:00 p.m., Maddux stated his official position on the matter to Barbara by knocking on her door and slipping inside to deliver the news—he was worried.

"Do we have any idea where he might be?" Maddux asked. "You don't think we're getting played again, do you?"

"In this world, I make no certain declarations, other than the fact that there really are no sure things," Barbara said.

"A bit ironic, don't you think?" Maddux asked.

She shrugged. "There's little room for irony in the world of espionage. Some things just are true, no matter how you might like to nuance them."

"Well, we need to figure out what's really going on here before we plot our next move."

Barbara nodded. "Do you know what the protocol is now?"

"I'll be downstairs," he said, giving her a knowing glance.

"Come get me if you need something. My involvement would only make things awkward for somebody."

"Understood."

Maddux walked downstairs to the hotel lobby, anxious to see if all the protocol he'd been instructed to follow would produce the results he needed when necessary.

He sauntered up to the bar and ordered a drink. Collecting the change, he went over to a pay phone and dialed the emergency number he'd been given for the CIA's Prague station chief.

"Verify your identity," a man said, answering the phone.

"Two roads diverged in a yellow wood and I—I took the one most traveled by."

"Identity verified," the man said. "Return to the dance floor, and someone will make contact with you there."

"Returning to the dance floor," Maddux said before hanging up.

Maddux went back to the bar and ordered another drink, consuming it much more slowly. After fifteen minutes, he went to the restroom and locked himself in the farthest stall.

As he was seated and pretending to do his business, Maddux heard a man enter the room and whistle the first few lines of Buddy Holly's big 1958 hit, *Peggy Sue*. Once the man stopped, Maddux picked right up where the man had left off, whistling the rest of the chorus. Seconds later, a sheet of paper slid beneath his stall, instructing him to go to the alleyway behind the hotel.

Maddux followed the instructions, and five minutes later found himself face to face with the Prague station chief, Roland Norton. With a hat pulled down low across his face and a Lucky Strike struggling to bear any more ashes, Norton shot quick glances in both directions before speak to Maddux.

"Nice night for a walk," Norton said.

"If you like jumping over puddles," Maddux replied with the specified phrase.

"Anybody follow you?" Norton asked, relaxing his shoulders for the first time since he came into contact with Maddux.

Maddux shook his head. "I'm clean from what I can tell."

"Either way, we better make this quick. I'd hate for anyone to see you talking with me. It could blow your cover. The StB will dig through every person I come in contact with and rake through your life until it's barely recognizable."

"Let's get on with it then."

"Without the asset, we seem to be in quite a predicament."

"Nothing we can't fix with a little bit of luck."

Norton checked over both shoulders. "It's going to take more than luck this time. We're going to need an extraction, if that's even possible."

"I'm sure Barbara and I can handle it."

Norton chuckled. "I like your bravado, rookie, but this isn't some training exercise. You don't even know where they're holding Voss."

"And you do?"

"One of my contacts reported earlier that the StB is taking him to a small interrogation camp just outside town. It's the same location they've used in the past to try and break our assets."

"And you're sure Voss hasn't flipped on us again just to save his own tail? We're not exactly talking about the most seasoned asset. In fact, he's spent far more time working for the KGB than for us."

"Voss planted the bugs for us—and they've already been confirmed they're working. So it's possible that his allegiance still lies with us. We can't be certain about anything in this business."

Maddux shook his head, a guarded smile spreading across his face. "Someone else told me that earlier today."

"You must spend plenty of time in wise company."

"Wise is one part of the word I'd use to describe her."

Norton chuckled. "I'm glad you two are getting along so well. Now, in terms of what steps to take next, I think there's a facility about eight kilometers just past the border that's worth taking a look at. The StB has been known to take prisoners there that it's trying to break."

"Our spy would likely be someone they are trying to jam into the category."

"Unless he's not really *our spy*."

With a scowl, Maddux eyed Norton closely.

"So you have an alternate theory?"

Norton shrugged. "Perhaps. It's also entirely possible that the StB set this whole thing up to help Voss gain better access to us and our intel. Consider how they allegedly recruited him. If they could dream that up and use a portion of that to develop his legend, I don't think they're above such a move."

"It's a possibility, but you really think Voss could pull that off? He's too—too . . ."

"Trusting? Kindhearted?" Norton asked.

Maddux nodded vigorously in agreement.

"That's what your file said about you until recently," Norton said. "You weren't tough enough to be an agent for us, but here you are. People change. Remember that. It's one of the most important things you must understand about people if you plan on succeeding in the world of espionage."

"Duly noted," Maddux said. "Now, what does your gut tell you is happening?"

"I don't trust my gut; I trust intel," Norton said. "Go stake out the camp, and get some actionable information. Barbara will know what to do."

Maddux grabbed Norton by the arm and handed him the sheet of paper that had been slipped into Maddux's pocket unknowingly.

September 12, 1952. *Lidové noviny*

"What's this?" Norton asked.

"I don't know," Maddux said. "But someone gave that to me before I left. Would you mind getting me the paper on that date and sending it to me in Bonn?"

Norton shrugged. "I'm not going to make any promises, but I'll see what I can do."

After thanking Norton, Maddux shoved his hands into his pockets and headed back to the hotel. He cast furtive glances over his shoulder before going upstairs and knocking on Barbara's door. As soon as she opened it, he rushed inside.

"What is it?" she asked.

Maddux locked the door behind him.

"They've detained Voss and taken him to an StB prison facility."

"And what does Norton want us to do about it?" she asked.

"He said you'd know what to do, but not before he said that we need to bring him back some actionable intel."

She put on her coat. "Grab your things. We've got to hurry. The longer this thing goes, the lower his chance of survival."

XV

MADDUX DROVE HALF AN HOUR outside of town while Barbara tinkered with several gadgets in her bag. She insisted Maddux drive while she set up some of the necessary devices. He continued to check his mirror for the possibility of any StB vehicles tailing him. For more than half the trip, he didn't see another vehicle, which made him feel uneasy in some respects. Deep down, he kept questioning if he was missing something in his rearview mirror.

A few headlights popped up behind him on long straightaways only to disappear for good at various intersections. Maddux noted that he didn't see another vehicle for the final five minutes, which was driven mostly along a dirt path leading to the prison.

"You about done?" Maddux asked.

Barbara tinkered with the radio in her hand, unscrewing the back and replacing the batteries.

"Almost," she said without looking up.

"You want to tell me what the plan is?"

"We're going to investigate any activity, and then we're going to eavesdrop."

"And if we find anything?"

"We'll call Pritchett and ask him what he wants us to do."

Maddux eyed her closely. "So, you're just going to ignore Norton?"

"He's here to support our mission, not to run the op. Pritchett is the one who will give us recommendations on how to proceed."

"Recommendations? As opposed to orders?"

"Define them how you wish," she said, tightening the screws on the back of the transistor radio. "I prefer not to place my life in the hands of anyone who isn't here on the ground with me—and even then I'm not very fond of trusting co-workers. In the end, you're going to find out that everyone is really out for themselves."

"I'm out for the truth," Maddux said.

"About your father, but the rest of it means very little to you."

"And you're on the moral high ground here?"

She chuckled. "Of course not. I never claim such territory. I just know how people are. They'll always disappoint you, if you let them."

"Do you trust me?"

She took a deep breath, exhaling slowly. "I could be persuaded, but the jury is still out on you, Maddux. You haven't been around here long enough for me to make a determination one way or another. But for now, I'm going to choose to think the best of you. How's that?"

"I'll take it," Maddux said, easing off the gas and onto the brake.

"Looks like we're here."

"Indeed we are," he said before turning off the main road and pulling behind a clump of trees and bushes that formed a natural blind.

"Well, let's get to work."

They climbed out of the car and hurriedly removed several devices designed to aid them in their reconnaissance work.

Maddux and Barbara both placed binoculars to their eyes and peered at the dimly lit open area shielded only by a chain-link fence. The detention facility sat more than 200 meters away. Lighted by only a handful of lampposts that barely extended above the top of the single-story barracks, the activity happening wasn't easy to make out. A pair of armed guards shoved one blindfolded prisoner across the premises. Struggling to stay on his feet, the captive finally fell headlong to the ground. When he did, the covering dropped around his neck, revealing more of his face.

"Do you see what I see?" Maddux asked.

"That's our asset—Otto Voss," she said softly. "What did you get yourself into, my friend?"

"Looks like his cover is blown," Maddux said, noting which building they took Voss into.

"More like his head is about to be blown off."

"We need to talk to Pritchett."

They both jumped back into their car and drove a few miles down the road until they came to a small grocer. Against the wall on the outside was a small payphone.

Maddux dialed Pritchett's secure number and fed the crowns into the slot until the line started ringing.

"Yes," Pritchett said as he answered.

"They have the asset," Maddux said.

"What's the weather?" Pritchett asked, engaging their coded conversation protocol.

"Cold and stormy," Maddux answered, conveying that the asset was detained and imprisoned.

"What's tomorrow's forecast?"

"Looks like the storm will be here for a while."

"Better take cover," Pritchett said, code for *come back home*. "That storm may only lull just to draw you into it. Trust the intel you gather, not necessarily what you see."

"You think the storm is trying to draw us in? I know what I saw."

"Like I said, you can't always trust what you see. Get as far away from the storm as possible."

Maddux hung up and returned to the car and re-hashed his coded conversation.

"What does your gut tell you?" Maddux asked Barbara.

"I'm not inclined to chase storms," she said. "And if Pritchett thinks they might be trying to set us up, there's no need to stick around. Plus, there's no good reason to fight for Voss. I think he's a snake in the grass."

"So you think that was all staged?"

She shrugged. "I doubt it. The StB doesn't seem that sophisticated to me, but I learned long ago not to underestimate my opponent. Nevertheless, they did nothing to ensure that we showed up here to see Voss frog marched across the courtyard. It seems legitimate to me."

"So, why not go get him?"

"I can think of a thousand reasons to leave him there."

"But we gave him our word—and he's in trouble."

"And he knows something about your father, doesn't he?"

Maddux sighed. "Maybe—I don't know, to be honest. Though, I really want to find out what else he knows."

"I can't fault you there," she said. "I'd move Heaven and Earth to find out what happened to my father if he went missing . . . But I wouldn't want to do it at the expense of others. There are limits to our curiosity in this business. Such insatiable inquisitiveness is a serious hazard to your health."

"Letting questions linger is also a serious hazard to your mental health," he said. "But I also feel like we owe it to him to try. Besides, he already did what we asked him to do, which was plant those listening devices."

"I'm not going to be able to stop you, am I?" she asked.

Maddux shook his head. "These bastards need to be stopped. And while I might still have some distrust for Voss, he deserves to have us pluck him from this sticky situation, if anything because we created it. So, are you on board?"

She stared out the car window for a brief moment before turning back to Maddux. "Okay, I'm in. But I'm going to need you to do me a favor."

"Anything," he said. "You just name it."

"Oh, I don't think you should say that so enthusiastically, especially with a smile on your face."

Maddux shrugged. "What are you going to make me do?"

A faint smile spread across her face as she looked skyward. "I've read your file—and I promise you won't like it."

XVI

MAA FEW MINUTES LATER, Maddux and Barbara were pushing their car back behind the natural blind and preparing for the next step in their mission. Maddux paused to glance at the StB detention facility through his binoculars, while Barbara dug through her tool kit. After a few seconds, she let out a triumphant exult when she found the contraption she had been searching for.

"Care to tell me what it is you want me to do yet?"

"You've got eyes on the facility, right?"

"Affirmative." He glanced at her and scowled. "You're avoiding my question."

She ignored his comment. "The only other thing we need then is to get ears there as well. Outside of being there, this is the next best thing."

"And how do you plan on doing that?"

"You're going to do it for me," she said, looking at him and then upward at the telephone pole.

"What is that look supposed to mean?" He paused for a second. "Oh, no. You don't mean? Wait. You read my file and you still want to make me do that? Are you that cruel?"

"You wouldn't be the first person to suggest that I was cruel, though I think this situation is slightly different. If you could do my job, I'd let you. But for the sake of time, it's quicker if you shimmy on up the pole instead of me."

"Come on."

"It's very simple, really. You just climb the telephone poll and find the right line so we can listen in on all their calls, both coming and going. Besides, maybe we'll intercept a real state secret."

"You mean something that might get us both promoted and out of this assignment?"

"Perhaps, but I've found everything about this case to be fascinating. The more you peel the layers back, the more intrigue is revealed. Meanwhile, you'll be one step closer to getting information about your father."

"Yeah," Maddux said. "If Voss dies, my father's memory dies with him. And I can't have that. Just point in the direction of where I'm supposed to go and how I do this."

She instructed him on how to attach the wires. Then she pointed up at the telephone pole situated just a few feet away.

"Get climbing," she said.

Why does it always have to be something so high in the air?

Maddux bit down on the wires and scurried up the pole. Once he reached the height of the line, he attached the wires and nodded down to Barbara. She fiddled with the dials for a few seconds and then held the headphones tight to her ears. Maddux eased his way down to the ground and watched Barbara's eyes.

"Anything yet?" he asked.

She held up her index finger as she stared off in the distance.

"This is the right line," she said, removing the left side of her headset. "I just heard one of the guards speaking with a superior about a shipment of prisoners tomorrow."

"Anything about Voss?"

"Not that I could tell. Just sit tight."

For the next half hour, Maddux sat in silence as Barbara recorded notes about every phone call that went in and out of the StB prison facility. In between calls, he asked Barbara why the CIA didn't eavesdrop in this manner more often. She explained that it was a high-risk operation and was only allowed during times of duress or other special circumstances.

"High risk?" Maddux asked. "This seems pretty low risk to me."

Seconds later, he heard a vehicle engine roaring in their direction. What followed was the sporadic movement of a spotlight, flashing toward them.

"Get down," Barbara said in a whisper, grabbing Maddux and pulling him low to the ground.

Maddux's chin rested on the dirt as he peered through the brush at the headlights now bearing down on their position.

"Still seem low risk to you?" she asked.

Maddux didn't say a word, instead watching intently as a Jeep approached and then stopped a few meters on the other side of the tree line.

Two armed guards hopped out and started combing the area. They shouted back and forth to one another in Czech. Just when they appeared to be heading back to their vehicle, one of the men stopped and turned to look over his shoulder. Maddux swore the man was looking right toward them. He spun all the way around and marched directly toward Maddux.

Barbara put her hand on Maddux's arm. He knew she was trying to keep him calm and anchored, but Maddux could tell if he didn't do something, they would be discovered. He took a deep breath and considered his options before making a move.

Leaping to his feet, Maddux pulled a knife out of his pocket and stabbed the man in the throat. The sudden commotion rattled the other guard, drawing his attention in the direction of the scuffle.

"Peter?" the other guard called as he rushed over to find out what was going on.

Waiting until the guard was stooped over and looking at his colleague, Maddux tried to jam his knife into the other guard. However, he reacted in enough time to thwart Maddux's attack, dropping his gun to stop Maddux's blade. The two men wrestled for a few seconds as Maddux's knife was stripped from his hand and slung into the darkness.

Maddux fought hard before getting pinned to the ground and suffering several wicked punches. Barbara scrambled toward the car, which arrested the man's attention briefly. Maddux figured the man was surprised by the fact he had more than one agent to deal with.

The guard's grip tightened around Maddux's throat before using Maddux's tie to choke him. Maddux struggled to break the man's grip before remembering Rose's special knife in the tie clip. He freed the tie clip and pressed a button that unleashed the blade. Then Maddux shoved the knife into the man's neck, causing him instinctively to release his grip and grab his neck instead. That was the small opening Maddux needed to break free and turn the tide of the fight.

Maddux rolled over on top of the man, who yelped in pain as blood gushed from his neck. A flurry of punches knocked him out, but Maddux didn't get up.

Barbara handed him another knife.

"Finish him off," she said. "We need to make sure he's gone and hide the bodies before other guards come looking for these two."

Maddux slashed the guard's neck and less than thirty seconds later, he was dead.

"Let's get them out of here," Barbara said.

Maddux and Barbara worked quickly, dragging the two dead guards into the bushes behind the tree line. Then they turned off the lights of the Jeep and pushed it into the bushes.

"They won't find this until sometime tomorrow," she said. "Hopefully that will be enough time to get Voss back."

"I'll finish this," Maddux said. "You listen in. We don't want to miss anything."

Maddux steered the guards' vehicle behind the brush and decided to push it down into a nearby ravine to save time, just in case they needed more of it. He watched as the Jeep tumbled down the hill.

Good luck finding that tomorrow.

For good measure, Maddux slung the guards' bodies down in the ravine as well. As the bodies bounced against the rocks toward the bottom, he considered what he'd just done for the first time. Killing was easier than he thought it would be, mostly because it was a kill-or-be-killed situation. He resolved never to be callous about killing another person, but these men whose lives he'd just snuffed out would've been unapologetic about killing him. Maddux had chosen this life now—and he couldn't escape all the baggage that accompanied it.

Before he could fully process all that had transpired, Barbara rushed toward him, whispering excitedly.

"I've got it! I've got it!" she said.

"Got what?"

"All the information about Voss. They're going to move him in the morning to a different facility."

"That sounds like our chance," Maddux said.

"Tomorrow at 6:00 a.m. they're moving a high-level prisoner per Mikhailov's orders."

"That has to be Voss."

"I agree."

"Let's get moving then. We've got an escape to plan."

* * *

MADDUX AND BARBARA RETURNED to their hotel to gather all their belongings and check out. They left their keys inside their hotel room along with full payment before they slipped out the backdoor to avoid watchful eyes. Once they were back inside their car, Maddux clutched the steering wheel with both hands and took a deep breath.

"Mind filling me in on your big plan?" Barbara asked.

"It's really simple," he began. "We take control of the vehicle escorting Voss to another facility, break him out, and go home."

"It's too simple."

"In the automotive industry, the engineers always say, 'The fewer moving parts, the better.'"

"Well, we aren't manufacturing cars, in case you haven't noticed."

"No, but we are crunched for time and resources. They're going to be moving Voss in a few hours, and we don't have time for an elaborate plot."

She tied her hair into a bun and stared out the window.

"Okay, let's just say your simple plan will work," she said. "How do you plan on stopping the transport?"

"I was thinking a small explosive device that we could set off underneath the front of the vehicle."

"And killing our asset? That's not the best idea."

"You got a better one?"

"How about I stand near a car that's broken down and play the role of the damsel in distress? I could put the hood up and pout like this."

She stuck out her bottom lip, pairing it with sad eyes.

"Almost irresistible," he said. "But there's no guarantee they'll stop. We need a sure thing. If we miss our shot, Voss will be gone for good."

"Fine," she said. "We'll do it your way. But if we fail, I'm letting you take the fall with Pritchett."

"And when I'm right, you're giving me full credit."

"Fair enough. Now, let's move to your next problem."

"Which is?"

"You need to make an explosive device that will disable their vehicle but not kill our asset. Any idea where you're going to get something like that at this time of night?"

"I've already thought of this—and I know just the place."

XVII

MADDUX DROVE ONTO THE ROAD, struggling to temper his instinct to press the accelerator to the floorboard. "Well, are you gonna tell me or keep me guessing?"

"Remember the plant we went to earlier today?"

She nodded. "The ones with all the armed guards?"

"That's the one. Everything we need is right there."

"So, now we need a plan to sneak into the plant. Have you thought about that, too?"

"I noticed an unguarded back entrance," he said. "There was a padlock around it, but I can pick it."

"And what about any guards patrolling the premises?"

"I can take care of them," he said. "You just stay ready with the car."

* * *

MADDUX MADE QUICK WORK of the padlock after they arrived at the manufacturing facility. He eased the gate open and crouched low as he stole across the commons area toward the main building. He moved along the wall toward the back entrance, identifying an opening he could reach with the help of a stack of nearby pallets and a short leap up to the ledge.

Just as Maddux prepared to climb, cigarette smoke wafted in his direction.

A Marlboro Man, huh. This shouldn't take too long. Mild as May.

Maddux crept up to the corner and put his head down, listening to the rhythm of the guard's steps draw near. Once certain the man was only a step away, Maddux swung his arm laterally and caught the guard in the throat. The man crumpled to the ground as he gasped, the cigarette toppling from his mouth. Maddux delivered a series of punches that knocked the man out. Pulling the body to the back of the building, Maddux used a couple of pallets to conceal the guard before climbing through a window and into the facility.

Maddux eased himself inside and hung from the ledge with his arms extended, giving himself a short three-foot drop. After he landed on the concrete floor, Maddux headed straight toward the section of the plant where he'd seen crates of materials. He figured it wouldn't take him long to put together a rudimentary device, something he'd learned to do during the war. But after prying open one of the crates, he realized he wouldn't have to.

You've got to be kidding me.

Maddux stared inside at the box's contents—land mines. He shoved several into his backpack and headed toward the window.

The click of a gun stopped him dead.

"Halt," a guard said.

Maddux lifted his arms in a gesture of surrender and

turned around slowly. The guard yelled to a colleague, who rushed over and handcuffed Maddux. They led him to a small office and bound him to a chair.

"An American?" the guard said. "Let's see what you have in your bag?"

He unzipped the bag, and his eyes bulged at the sight of Maddux's loot. With a wide grin, the guard wagged his index finger at Maddux. "You shouldn't have done that," the guard said before turning to his colleague. "Call it in."

XVIII

VOSS HAD STRUGGLED to stay conscious before succumbing to the exhaustion of torture and collapsing onto his cell floor. A loud clank down the hall startled him awake, leaving him in a disoriented state. Without a window or a watch for reference, Voss was left guessing what time it was—or even what day it was. The yellow fluorescent bulbs in the corridor flickered, scarcely suppressing the darkness.

Voss wiped off the side of his face only to stop abruptly. The dried blood that had spidered across his cheek had also collected dirt, likely when he was lying on the ground passed out. Voss gently ran his fingers along his cheeks, feeling the newly formed contours from the mingled mess clinging to his face. After repeating the process a few times, he looked down at his hands and noticed fresh blood. It hadn't fully stopped oozing from the beatings he suffered when he was first apprehended by Mikhailov.

Lost in the pain, Voss didn't notice the dust rolling across him from the four pairs of boots now surrounding him. He looked up to see Mikhailov and a trio of guards peering downward.

Mikhailov crouched low, getting eye level with Voss. "There's some good news and bad news," Mikhailov began. "Which one would you like to hear first?"

Voss returned his gaze to the floor and shrugged.

"Well, which one will it be?" Mikhailov bellowed. "It's important for my delivery."

"Dealer's choice," Voss said.

Mikhailov growled. "Then it's good news first for you."

"I'm listening," Voss said, his voice barely rising above a whisper.

"You're being transferred out of here soon," Mikhailov said. "Some poor misguided souls happen to believe that you are of some value to them in the near future. But I would caution you against getting comfortable in their presence. They are a fickle lot."

"And the bad news?"

"You're being transferred out of here soon, but not so soon that I can't finish what we started earlier," Mikhailov said. He followed his statement with a swift kick from his steel-toed boot into Voss's ribs.

Voss yelped, doubling over in pain. "Just kill me now."

Mikhailov threw his head back and howled with laughter. "Now why would I do that? This is far too much fun."

Another kick. Then out came a cropping stick. One strike after another sent Voss rolling across the dirt. He didn't go far before he bumped up against a pair of legs. Voss headed in the other direction in an effort to avoid another whip from Mikhailov. But the short-term reprieve from pain was offset by how angry Mikhailov grew from Voss's defiance.

"Don't run away from me, you vermin," Mikhailov said as he finally stilled Voss and put a boot heel on his throat.

"Just do it—just kill me," Voss pleaded again.

"Oh, no," Mikhailov said. "This is far too much fun—and all well-deserved at your expense, you traitor."

Up and down Voss's body, Mikhailov struck his helpless prisoner.

"Do you think this is a game to me?" Mikhailov bellowed.

Voss curled up in a fetal position and covered his head with his hands.

"No—it's—not," Mikhailov said, emphasizing each word with a kick to Voss's back.

Voss winced with each blow, wondering how long the abuse would last, speculating how much more he could take. The thought crossed his mind more than once of leaping to his feet and attacking Mikhailov just so the madman would end the ordeal. Voss concluded a bullet to the head would be merciful, a shot Mikhailov would willingly take if he felt threatened enough.

But Voss never had the chance to discover the limits of his pain as Mikhailov stopped and paced around the room.

"You have done little to help your new country in her fight against the bullies from the west," Mikhailov said. "And then I learn that you are instead betraying your country. At least being ambivalent toward Czechoslovakia would have been forgivable. But now? You have committed treason to one of the few countries in the world that would accept you. We welcomed you in with open arms, and this is how you repay us?" Mikhailov spat on Voss's head. "You're not worth any more of my time," Mikhailov said. "Someone else will finish you off. I find spending a bullet on you to be a waste, though you certainly don't deserve to live. But someone else will determine your fate. I have far more important issues to attend to."

Voss heard Mikhailov's footsteps as he plodded toward the door.

"What about my family?" Voss said after rolling over.

Mikhailov stopped at the door and spun around. "What about them?"

"What are you going to do to them?"

"That remains to be seen, but perhaps you should have considered that before you acted so recklessly. Goodbye, Otto Voss."

The cell door clanked hard behind Mikhailov, leaving Voss to ponder his chances of survival.

XIX

MADDUX FELT THE SWEAT bead up on his forehead and trickle down his face. He was powerless to stop it as some streaks wormed their way into the corner of his eyes, burning them. In an effort to ward the sweat away, Maddux squinted hard and blinked repeatedly. He hoped when he fully opened his eyes again that the guards would be gone. But they weren't.

The nightmare was very real.

The guard who'd been watching Maddux nodded toward his colleague. The other guard picked up the phone and dialed a number. But he stopped and frowned. He pulled the receiver away from his ear and stared at the phone.

"It's not working," he said. "The line is dead."

"Try another line in the other office."

The man scurried off.

"Are you aware of what you're guarding here?" Maddux said. "There are very dangerous and volatile weapons located here. Under the right conditions, this place could explode—and you right along with it."

"It is so dangerous that you broke into this building

and stole some of those same weapons," the guard said as he chuckled. "You must think I'm a fool."

"I never said that," Maddux said. "But you are making a big mistake."

"And why's that?"

"Because I'm going to kill you."

The guard belted out a hearty laugh. "You are handcuffed and tied to a chair. Killing me won't be easy. But I will let you live in your delusion."

Moments later, the other guard returned. "The phones are down in every office."

"Go to his house and bring him down here so we'll know what to do with this arrogant American."

The other guard nodded and quickly disappeared down the hall.

Maddux waited while plotting his next move. Though he hadn't anticipated such a situation, Rose had. "Would you mind getting me something to drink? I'm really thirsty."

The guard sneered at Maddux. "I won't fall for your tricks, you stupid American."

Maddux shrugged. "It's not a trick. I'm simply thirsty."

"Thirst will be the least of your worries when my fellow co-worker returns with our boss in about fifteen minutes."

Fifteen minutes? Stay calm. Don't panic.

The guard stood directly in front of Maddux, about ten feet away. "Why so pale, Mr. Tough Guy?"

Maddux set his jaw and took a deep breath.

Here it goes.

He pointed his right foot up at the guard's chest and

then stomped hard on his back heel.

Nothing.

The guard stopped and stared incredulously at Maddux before breaking into a laugh.

"What are you doing? Stomping your foot? Are you throwing a temper tantrum?"

The guard didn't move, except to laugh at Maddux, who repeatedly stomped his heel against the ground.

Still nothing.

Rose, what did you do?

Maddux tried once more, swiftly forcing his heel to the ground while keeping his toes pointed at the guard's chest.

The bullet that tore through the front of Maddux's shoe barely made a sound. The guard staggered backward and tumbled to the ground as the shot hit him in the chest. He gasped for breath and muttered something.

Maddux stood, hunched over in an awkward position with his legs still tethered to the chair. Shuffling toward a nearby support beam, he beat the chair against the pole until the chair splintered. Once he untied himself, Maddux used one of the tricks he learned from Elmer Sellers to escape the handcuffs.

Maddux snatched his bag off the floor near the dying guard and grabbed several more mines before exiting the building. He raced toward the fence where Barbara awaited him. Grinning and holding a pair of bolt cutters, Barbara had removed a human-sized portion of the fence, which was more than enough for Maddux to squeeze through.

"I thought I told you to stay in the car," Maddux said.

She hustled after him toward their running vehicle. "You didn't say to stay *in* the car," she said. "You just said that I stay *ready* with the car. I think I'm ready. Don't you?"

Maddux gave her a sideways glance and climbed into the driver's side.

"You can thank me for cutting the phone line, too," she said after slamming the passenger side door shut.

"Good work," Maddux said. "You saved my hide back there."

"Now, next time, let's not make any assumptions about how simple a mission is going to be—because they're never going to be simple."

"Save the lecture for later. We've got to hurry up and plant these mines or else we're going to lose Voss forever."

"Don't you worry," Barbara said. "If we just so happen to survive, I'll have a full-blown lecture for you. I might even wait until we are both seated in Pritchett's office before I give it. But make no mistake about it, the lecture is coming."

"Do you know how to set landmines?" Maddux asked.

"I've set my share in the past. Don't worry. I know what I'm doing."

"I wasn't worried. You've made it abundantly clear through your actions—and words—that you know how to handle yourself in the field. But we need to make sure we're on the same page here. Communication is vital if we're going to pull this off."

She gave him a steely-eyed glare. "You just worry about how you're going to position the mines in the road so you don't blow our asset up and we'll be just fine."

Maddux stomped his foot on the gas as their car sped through Prague and back toward the prison facility.

"We've got less than hour, which I hope is enough time."

"It won't be," Barbara said flatly. "It never is."

A flash of lightning struck a tree sitting on a nearby ridge. The brilliant light blinded Maddux for a moment. He shook his head in an attempt to rid the image seared into his eyes.

"We have no choice," Maddux said. "We're gonna have to make it work."

XX

AS MADDUX AND BARBARA approached the StB detention facility, Maddux stopped their car and informed his partner that he needed to do something. Then he stole across the yard of a nearby home and found a motorcycle. Pushing it toward the road, Maddux instructed Barbara to hide the car near a field a half-mile up the road.

"What do you think you're doing?" she asked while glaring at him. "This was not part of your simple plan. Are you aware how much unneeded attention we're going to attract when we steal that motorcycle?"

"We're not going to steal it," he said. "We're only going to borrow it."

"I doubt the owners will see it that way."

"If we leave it for them, I'm sure they won't be too upset. Miffed, maybe, but not anything to call the police about. They'll just assume some kids were having fun at their expense."

"Those are grand assumptions. It's also just as realistic to assume that they get angry and come out with guns blazing."

"It's four-thirty in the morning," Maddux said. "I'm betting that nobody is leaving for work in the next two hours."

"You better be right about this or else you're going to foil a good plan."

Maddux grinned. "So you think this plan isn't just simple, but that it's good?"

"Don't press your luck," Barbara said, shoving him in the chest playfully.

"I'm glad you agree. Now go hide the car and then come back down this way. I'll be pushing the bike so we don't wake the owners up."

"Finally, you're thinking with your brain."

"I never stopped."

Maddux slung his backpack over his shoulder and positioned himself on the right side of the motorcycle. He held the handlebars and pushed the bike along the side of the road. Glancing up at the sky, he noticed how bright the stars were even with a moon to steal some of their thunder. He took note of the crickets chirping and enjoyed the calming sounds of a brook trickling along its course. The reprieve helped Maddux gather his thoughts and prepare for the tricky task ahead.

Several minutes later, Barbara caught up with him on foot.

"It's hidden," she said. "Now do you mind telling me why we just had to steal this bike?"

"Options," Maddux said. "We're behind enemy lines here, and we need every alternate escape route possible."

She cast a furtive glance at him. "Where did you learn that?"

"In my paratrooper training," Maddux said. "That

was one of the first things we learned to do once we hit the ground—find as many exit routes as quickly as you can. Once you have a way to survive, then you can get on with the business of catching your enemy off guard."

"Impressive," she said. "I learned that in my training, too, though I never considered stealing a motorcycle as an exit strategy if I wasn't forced to do so in the moment."

Maddux winked at her and smiled. "We might still make a good team just yet, almost as good as me and Rose."

Barbara sighed. "Why'd you have to bring her up and ruin the moment? You have a thing for her, don't you?"

Maddux wasn't biting. "Let's talk about our plan for capturing Voss back from the StB, shall we?"

Barbara rolled her eyes. "You're not very good at subtleties, are you?"

Maddux ignored her comment. "So, this road is mostly comprised of dirt which makes it easy for us to hide these mines. We don't have time to test them, but I figure if we dig down a few inches beneath the surface, we should still be able to get plenty of pressure necessary to detonate the device. What do you think?"

"Yes, it doesn't have to be deep at all," she said. "Many of these mines have hairline triggers. Just the slightest pressure and they'll explode. They're particularly dangerous to set."

Maddux stopped and held his finger in the air.

"What is it?" she asked.

"You hear that?"

She nodded.

"Sounds like a transport vehicle," Maddux said. "We need to move."

They scrambled off the side of the road and hid in the bushes while waiting for the truck to pass. After half a minute, a large truck rumbled past them.

"Think that's Voss's ride?" Barbara asked.

"I'd be willing to bet everything I owned that that's it."

"We need to get to work."

"You can say that again," Maddux said.

He scurried onto the road with Barbara right beside him as the two of them got to work. He used a little bit of water from his canteen to soften the dirt and then dug beneath the surface. Barbara joined him, instructing him to keep the mines less than six inches apart so that even the best driver couldn't maneuver through the field they'd set up.

When they finished, Maddux stood and dusted off his hands. He crept back toward the edge of the road and put his hands on his hips, surveying their work.

"After you're done admiring your job, I need you to do me a favor," Barbara said, holding out a pair of wires.

Maddux reluctantly took the wires and sighed. "You want me to climb the pole again, don't you?"

Barbara smiled and patted him on the arm. "Do be a dear and get to climbing."

Less than a minute later, Maddux was stationed high on the pole, while Barbara listened in on the line.

"Anything yet?" Maddux said.

She shook her head.

Maddux glanced at his watch—a quarter till six. He peered off into the distance at the StB facility, where there seemed to be some stirring in the commons area. With sunrise approaching, he hoped that the Czech secret police would move Voss under the guise of night.

An operation requiring this much firepower during the daytime could increase the chances of eyewitnesses, not to mention the likelihood of getting apprehended before escaping across the border.

"Wait a minute," Barbara said. "I'm getting something. They're getting ready to transport the prisoner and informing the other StB facility that they need to be ready to receive him."

"Excellent," Maddux said. "Can I get down now?"

Barbara held up her finger. "Wait."

Maddux's arms tingled, losing most of the sensation in them. "I need to take a break soon."

She looked up at him. "You can climb down now. We have some things to discuss."

Maddux slid down the pole.

"What is it?" he said, handing the wires back to Barbara.

"It's Voss. They requested medical personnel to be on hand when he arrives. Apparently, he's taken quite a beating."

Maddux gazed at the facility in the distance and set his jaw. "Maybe we'll return the favor."

He watched the taillights on the transport vehicle spring on, followed by the headlights.

"It's time," Maddux said. "They're coming."

XXI

MADDUX AND BARBARA HUNCHED LOW in the bushes along the side of the road while waiting for the prison transport to rumble past. He peered through his binoculars as the truck spun around and eased toward the gate. A guard inspected the papers a driver handed over before giving the signal to raise the arm, allowing the truck to drive through.

"It won't be long now," Maddux said, following the transport with his binoculars.

"You sure this is going to work?" Barbara asked.

"I'm never completely sure of anything, but I am fairly confident that if we don't move quickly, we're not going to get very far. Those guards are going to hear the explosions and come after us. We just need to buy enough time to get us back to the main roads and blend in to traffic before they see us."

"I agree. Everything has to be done fast and with precision, starting with those land mines."

"If everything goes as planned, just take the motorcycle and go get the car as soon as it's safe. Then bring it back here. We should have just enough time to do that.

The prison transport should effectively block not only the road but also the guards' field of view. If we can get out of here without getting seen, we can blend right in and avoid getting arrested."

"We're going to be cutting it close."

Maddux nodded. "If you had a better plan, the time to speak up would've been hours ago."

"No, it's not that," she said. "I just always get nervous right before it comes time to execute something I've planned on doing for a while. But don't worry—I wasn't trying to imply anything. Just normal second-guessing."

"Let's focus," Maddux said. "We certainly shouldn't be voicing regret before we've even given the plan a chance."

"Agreed," she said, maintaining her focus on the road.

The sound of the approaching vehicle resulted in an elevated heart rate for Maddux. He was more excited than nervous, though he considered for a moment just how twisted such thoughts would've seemed to anyone else.

Am I wrong for looking forward to engaging in combat? Especially when my life will be on the line?

Maddux decided against delving into a psychoanalysis of his personality, realizing the current op required his full attention.

"Here they come," he whispered to Barbara.

Maddux watched as the wheels rolled over one of the mines.

Nothing.

What's happening?

Then the back wheels neared the line, which was

Maddux's greatest fear—the mines don't detonate once making contact with the front wheels instead exploding beneath the back wheels.

Nothing again.

Barbara looked at Maddux.

"What now?"

Maddux hopped up and ran toward the motorcycle. "Come on. We don't have much time."

XXII

MADDUX PATTED THE SEAT of the motorcycle and gestured for Barbara to hurry. She hustled after him, slogging through the high weeds. He looked through his binoculars at the detention facility, where all signs of bustling life had vanished.

Barbara crossed her arms and let out an exasperated sigh. "What do you expect to do now?"

He studied her closely before glancing down at the bike. "Can you drive one of these things?"

"I used to race these things," she said.

"Okay, save that story for later because I must hear it. For now, you get us as close as you can to that truck."

"This is your backup plan?"

"It'll work. Trust me."

"Just like those land mines?"

Maddux nodded toward the bike. "We can fight later, but we need to get moving."

Barbara hopped on the bike and kickstarted it. She needed several attempts before it coughed and wheezed to life. "You should've stolen a better bike."

"*Borrowed* a better bike," Maddux said as he climbed

on behind her.

"Hold on tight," she said before revving the accelerator and releasing the clutch.

The motorcycle lurched forward, the engine whining as Barbara worked her way up the gears. In less than a minute, the transport vehicle came into view.

"Just get me up close," Maddux said loudly into her ear.

"Then what?" she shouted.

"Go get the car."

She nodded and eased the motorcycle up against the bumper of the truck. Maddux tapped her on the shoulder and pointed forward, gesturing for her to keep moving. The message was received as she twisted the accelerator forward.

As they neared the truck, Maddux surveyed the passenger's side door for a place to grab onto the vehicle. The large mirrors on the side served as the perfect handle to steady himself before opening the door and assaulting the driver.

"Closer," Maddux said in Barbara's ear.

She followed orders, edging right up to the door.

Maddux grabbed on and gave Barbara a quick salute. She peeled off and spun around, leaning the bike to one side as she watched the unfolding scene. A few seconds later, she went off in the opposite direction back toward the car.

Meanwhile, Maddux prepared himself to take over the truck. He glanced in the window and saw the driver attempting to train his handgun on the intruder. The bumpy road increased the difficulty for the driver as well as for Maddux. Several pot holes launched the men up in the air for a short spell before they crashed back down to earth, the truck along with them. The driver fired a pair of shots, the first one shattering the window, the second one failing to even graze Maddux.

The driver returned both hands to the wheel while navigating a hard right curve. Seizing the opportunity, Maddux swung the door open and climbed inside, slamming the door behind him. The move frustrated the driver, whose gaze bounced between the road and his new passenger. The driver jerked the steering wheel to the left and then right in an effort to throw Maddux off balance, but it didn't stop him.

Maddux lunged for the driver's hand, yanking his gun onto the floorboard. The road straightened out, but the driver struggled to maintain a straight tact due to the assault. Maddux grabbed the right side of the wheel with his left hand before delivering a vicious uppercut to the driver's face. Though he put up some resistance with a few wild swings, Maddux asserted his will, punching the man twice more in the face before catching him with a chop to his throat. With the man clutching his throat, Maddux reached across the man's lap and opened the door. Seconds later, he tumbled out of the driver's side seat when Maddux used both his feet to shove the man into the ditch.

Maddux slammed on the brakes, causing the vehicle to skid to a complete stop. He scrambled onto the floorboard and snatched the driver's gun. Scaling the truck, Maddux shimmied slowly across the top and positioned himself above the backdoor, awaiting one of the guards to emerge.

The top of the first head he saw was Voss's, which

Maddux realized was a smart move if the truck had been surrounded by itchy trigger fingers. But it wasn't. The only person there was a patient Maddux.

Maddux waited until the guard's head was out in the open before shooting him. He crumpled to the ground, immediately drawing out a second guard, who edged out much more warily. Maddux waited until the man's head had emerged from the truck before taking aim from above. However, the gun jammed, the vacant click drawing the guard's attention.

Maddux dropped to the top of the truck and lay prone for several seconds before rolling off the passenger's side. Hitting the ground with a thud, Maddux hustled to the back of the truck in search of the first guard's weapon. But it wasn't there, instead slung over the back of the guard scanning the area.

Slipping into the wooded area on the other side of the road, Maddux regrouped to plan his next move. Without a weapon that could be used from afar, Maddux's success rested in his ability to surprise the remaining guard. Whatever Maddux did, he needed to do it with precision. Otherwise, he would be in trouble.

Maddux glanced over at Voss, who sat on the extended bumper of the truck with his hands and feet shackled. With a subtle nod Maddux wasn't sure could be seen, he managed to send what he hoped was an assuring message to a bloodied and beaten Voss.

With a barely discernible head bob in response, Voss eased into the truck.

Maddux crouched low as he crept sideways toward the front of the vehicle. He picked up a rock and tossed it in the opposite direction, drawing the attention of the guard. With his back to the truck, he kept his gun trained on the darkness surrounding him. Maddux sprinted toward the guard, drilling him from the side with a flying leap before he tumbled to the ground. Though the man's eyes remained closed, Maddux delivered two more punches to the face for good measure.

"Do you think they could recognize you?" Voss asked as he emerged from the behind the truck.

Maddux shook his head as he looked up at the scientist.

"My god, what did they do to you?" Maddux asked in disbelief at Voss's battered body.

"I'll survive," Voss said.

Their conversation ended when a pair of headlights roared up behind them. Maddux knelt and grabbed the gun from the most recently dispatched guard.

"It's me," Barbara said, holding her hands up in the air. "Now, get in."

Maddux unhooked the keys from the guard and released Voss, who rubbed his wrists and remained still.

"We need to do something about this mess," Maddux said.

Barbara rushed over and helped him toss the guards' bodies into the back before Maddux used a padlock to seal it. Then he drove the truck through a nearby field and parked it behind a thick tree line.

Sprinting toward the car, Maddux stopped just short of the passenger side door. He noticed Barbara standing outside, her arms crossed and a scowl on her face. Next he glanced at Voss, who hadn't moved since Maddux freed him.

"What's going on here?" Maddux asked.

"Why don't you ask our asset?" Barbara said. "I'd love to hear him try to explain this again."

"Otto, what's wrong?" Maddux asked.

The scientist exhaled slowly and kept his gaze focused on the ground. "I'm not going anywhere unless you make me a promise."

Maddux nodded. "Sure, Otto, anything. You name it."

"Shouldn't we wait until we hear his demands before agreeing to anything?" Barbara asked.

Voss waved dismissively with the back of his hand and said nothing, refusing to budge.

"We really need to get going," Maddux said. "If we wait around here much longer, they're going to catch up with us. You know as well as anyone that if we get caught, it won't be good for us."

In the distance, Maddux heard the rumbling of vehicles. Unable to see the compound any more, he relied on his instincts and heightened senses to tell him what was happening. But he didn't need anything to alert him to the impending doom they all faced if a truck's headlights caught them.

"Come on, Otto," Maddux said. "We don't have time for games. We both stuck our necks out for you."

"You shouldn't have," Voss said, still standing pat. "They're going to kill my wife and daughter if I escape, that much I'm sure of."

"We can contact the agency and send body guards," Maddux said. "We can protect them."

"No. No, you can't," Voss said with a growl.

"Our superior warned us not to come after you," Maddux said. "He told us to leave you—that bringing you home would be risky and he didn't want to lose a pair of agents. But here we are, defying his orders. At least give us a chance."

The engine in the distance was getting closer. Maddux estimated that if they weren't gone within the next minute, they would all be apprehended and tortured. And no one would come for them.

"There is one way to make sure that my family stays safe," Voss said as his eyes met Maddux's.

"Hurry it up," Barbara said. "We're running out of time."

"I will go with you if you promise to do something for me," Voss said.

Maddux noticed headlights had struck the trees down the road where it bent to the right.

"What do you want us to do?" Maddux asked.

"We need to get in the car or we'll all be dead in a matter of minutes," Barbara said.

"Come on now," Maddux said.

Voss hobbled toward the car and climbed into the back, sliding into the special hidden compartment nestled in the trunk. Maddux left the door open so they could communicate with Voss along with creating a more comfortable ride for their asset.

Stomping on the gas, Maddux sent dirt flying as he tried to avoid getting spotted by the vehicle coming down the road behind them. He glanced in his rearview mirror and shuddered when the lights struck the back of their car. Maddux rounded a corner and skidded to a halt at a railroad crossing. A locomotive tugging more than fifty rail cars eased along the tracks, the wheels squeaking as it did.

Barbara looked over her shoulder at the car that had come to a stop behind them.

"Great," she muttered. "We're done now."

The driver's side door flung open and a man sauntered up next to Maddux's window. He motioned for Maddux to roll it down, and he obliged.

"Good morning," the man said in Czechoslovakian. "How are you?"

"Never better," Maddux said, positioning himself between the man and Voss. "Is there a problem?"

"There might be for you if you don't get your taillight fixed," the man said with a smile. "Have a good day."

Maddux watched as the man returned to his vehicle and then turned left onto another dirt road that ran parallel to the tracks.

"That was close," Barbara said, letting out a sigh of relief.

The caboose passed by their position, allowing Maddux to drive over the tracks and continue on their way.

"So, how exactly can we keep your family safe?" Maddux asked.

"We must kill Gregory Mikhailov, the man who tortured me and tried to force me into a life of espionage," Voss said.

Barbara laughed nervously. "Are you out of your mind?"

"I'm afraid I'm not," Voss said. "And you must keep your word. Otherwise, you will have just condemned my family to death."

Maddux looked at Barbara, who pursed her lips and slowly shook her head.

"We can't do this, Ed," she said. "Do you know how much trouble we'll get into? This could start an international incident."

"Not if we were never there," Maddux said.

She huffed through her nose. "And you expect a man who's barely alive in our trunk to take on Mikhailov and kill him? You're crazier than you look."

"I didn't say I wouldn't help him, but I said as long as we were never there—as far as the Czechs know."

"This plan of yours should be interesting," she said with a hint of sarcasm.

"He doesn't need to plan this," Voss said from the back. "I know exactly how to do it, but we must hurry because it will be impossible once daylight breaks."

"Mind giving us a clue as to how you intend to kill him?" Barbara said.

"I don't really need much of your help," he said. "I just need one of the guard's guns, a piece of paper, and five minutes."

Maddux pressed the accelerator to the floor. "I think we can do that."

XXIII

THE ENGINE HUMMED as Maddux and company roared through downtown Prague before the workday began in earnest. The traffic was almost non-existent as he navigated the surface streets on the way to the home of Otto Voss's torturer. The sun had yet to fully rise out of the east when they parked along the street outside Gregory Mikhailov's house.

Maddux turned around and stared back at Voss, who was still wedged into the secret compartment.

"Are you still sure you want to do this?" Maddux asked.

"I've thought of nothing else for the past few days," Voss said. "If I don't, Mikhailov will simply victimize someone else. He must be stopped."

"Make this quick," Maddux said, handing over a gun to Voss. "If anyone sees us out here and reports us, our cover is blown. We can't have that, as you might well understand."

Voss nodded. "It'll be quick. I promise."

Maddux and Barbara took Voss by his arms and yanked him out of the trunk and into the car. He struggled to gain his balance once Barbara opened the door and led him out.

"Are you sure you don't need help?" Maddux asked again, wincing as he watched Voss attempt to walk.

"I'll be fine," Voss said as he glanced over his shoulder at the car.

Then he turned his full attention to the house in front of him before lumbering up the steps to confront his tormentor.

* * *

OTTO VOSS NARROWED HIS EYES and kept his head down as he imagined how he was going to kill Mikhailov. Voss first pictured himself simply barging through the front door and firing without a word, concluding that nothing needed to be said. Mikhailov was a monster, and the sooner the man's miserable life was ended, the better. But Voss decided that wasn't enough, instead concluding that Mikhailov needed to know why he was about to die. Reconsidering that approach, Voss concluded that handling Mikhailov in that way would not truly allow him to feel all the physical pain he thrust upon people who he'd incarcerated.

He needs to suffer.

Voss jiggled the knob on the front door, which barely moved.

Locked.

Voss muttered a string of expletives underneath his breath before summoning all his strength and kicking at the door. Once it flung open, Voss marched through it and called out for Mikhailov.

"Gregory Mikhailov," Voss declared, "it is past time for you to pay for all you've done."

Before Mikhailov entered the room, a young girl around the age of seven or eight emerged from around the corner toting a rag doll.

"What did my father do?" she asked.

Voss scowled at her. "Go back to bed, little girl. You don't want to see this."

"What are you going to do?" she asked.

For a fleeting moment, Voss considered telling her that he was going to kill her father. But he decided against it. "I'm going to shake your father's hand and tell him what a good man he is."

He hated lying to children, but it was a necessary evil at the moment. However, Voss didn't consider everything he said a complete lie. Despite his incessant manipulation of the facts, Voss decided he could state with integrity that he had thought Mikhailov was a good man and had actually shook his hand before he became famous. But that was a long time ago.

Voss's intentions were vastly different than what he said to Mikhailov's daughter. Voss loathed his tormentor—and all that he stood for. But he resolved to fake his affection for Mikhailov to earn the girl's trust.

"Where is your father?" Voss asked

"Come on. I'll show you," the girl said, taking Voss's arm and tugging on it.

"Lead the way," Voss said.

They wove through the house until they reached Mikhailov's room.

"He's in there," the girl said, nodding toward the door. "But I don't want to be here when he comes out."

Voss turned and eyed her closely.

"Then you better make yourself scarce," he said,

placing his hand on the door knob.

The girl disappeared down the hall, skipping away and humming a popular pop song.

Voss barged into Mikhailov's bedroom, only to find it unoccupied and likely never slept upon very often.

From the corner of the room, the sound of a slow clap emerged. Mikhailov sat in a plush chair, propping his right foot up on his left knee.

"The moment I heard you'd escaped, I knew you'd be headed straight here," Mikhailov said, brandishing his gun that had been resting in his lap. "I considered getting out of town for a few days, but I realized it was far more important to make an example out of you. Now, drop the weapon."

Voss complied, shaking his head and laughing nervously. "So, you're going to make a sport out of my death?"

"Don't act so high and mighty," Mikhailov said. "As the Americans say, if the shoe were on the other foot . . ."

"Americans at least show some compassion, even toward their enemies," Voss said with a growl.

"Then you would've fit right in there—if only you didn't have to die first." Mikhailov raised his pistol and pointed it straight at Voss's head.

"I've been waiting to do this for a long time," Mikhailov said before calling loudly. "Boys, there's something you need to see—the price for ignoring authority and doing whatever you wish."

The clatter of feet was followed by complete silence as two pairs of boys lined up in an effort to watch the spectacle. Slack-jawed, they stared at the unfolding situation.

Voss narrowed his eyes and looked up. "Children don't need to see this."

"Unruly ones do," Mikhailov said. "They need to see what happens when they defy their authorities again and again. I'm not always so cold, but people like you? I make all traitors suffer."

"I'm not a traitor," Voss said. "If anything, I'm trying to encourage others to take a stand to do the right thing no matter what."

"No matter what?" Mikhailov said. "I'd love to see how that pans out."

"You're free to give me the opportunity," Voss said. "It doesn't have to end this way."

Voss glanced down at Mikhailov's gun lying on the floor and chuckled.

"What's so funny?" Mikhailov demanded.

"It's nothing," Voss said before trying to keep a straight face.

"You're right, it doesn't have to end this way," Mikhailov said. "It's going to end far worse than you ever imagined."

Voss mustered up all the gumption he had and prepared to strike out at Mikhailov, even if that meant these actions would be the last thing Voss would ever do. But his actions ended abruptly as two teenaged girls stormed into the room, unaware of the situation unfolding.

"Father, do you have any cash?" asked one of the girls, ignoring Voss's presence.

Both girls stepped forward and held out their hands in anticipation of receiving money. It took a few seconds before they realized their father had trained his gun on someone else in the room.

Mikhailov glared at them.

"Can't you see that I'm busy?" he said.

Voss quickly slid behind the girls, using them to shield himself from Mikhailov.

"Let's come this way," Voss said, placing his arms around their shoulders and walking them backward toward the door.

With Mikhailov staring mouth agape at his former captive's brazen exit, Voss kept the girls positioned between him and Mikhailov in case the madman stormed into the hallway and had other ideas. In a matter of seconds, Voss stood on the front porch with Mikhailov's young daughter.

"Give this to your dad," Voss said to the girl, handing her a piece of paper. "He'll know what it means."

Voss hobbled back toward their car, which was parked around the corner. He slid into the secret compartment and yelled for Maddux to drive.

"What did you do?" Maddux asked.

"Not what I came here intending to do," Voss said.

"So you didn't kill him?" Barbara asked.

"Not yet," Voss said. "I just couldn't, not with his children all around. Besides, he got the upper hand on me and forced me to drop my weapon. His children are actually why I'm still alive."

"We need to disappear," Maddux said. "If anyone saw us . . ."

"They didn't," Barbara said. "I was watching. Nobody came out of that house except for Voss, and I didn't see any other nearby neighbors milling around."

"We still need to be careful," Maddux warned. "If even one person saw us in the vicinity and reported our car to the StB, we might not have such an easy time getting out of the country."

XXIV

ONCE MADDUX REACHED the main highway leading out of Prague, he shifted gears and pressed heavily on the gas. He remained tense as he wove in and out of traffic. Barbara put her hand on his shoulder and gave it a little squeeze.

"You might want to slow down," she said. "We don't want to attract any unwanted attention and get back on the StB's radar."

"You think they stopped watching us?" he asked.

"Not on purpose. But I think we lost them based on the fact that we haven't been arrested yet."

"Who knows? Maybe they'll have a surprise for us at the border. I wouldn't put anything past these bastards."

Maddux eased off the gas and glanced over at Barbara, whose gaze remained fixated on the road.

"What do you think happened back there?" she asked.

"He had the look of a shaken man, not a murderous one. He probably lost his nerve."

"That would be difficult to do if I were him,

especially with the way Mikhailov abused his family."

"I agree, but something hasn't added up to me this whole time about this situation."

"What do you mean?"

"Well, Voss's wife just seemed to go along with everything. In my experience, women often aren't so easily coerced."

"They are if their child's life is at stake. Never underestimate a mother's resolve to protect her children."

He shrugged. "Maybe that's it, but something about this hasn't set right with me since I was first briefed on this operation."

Barbara laughed softly. "You're starting to develop real agent instincts."

"Is that what you think this is?"

She nodded. "It's called cynicism. And if you work in the field long enough, you'll start to realize why you're never inclined to trust anyone. However, I must warn you that it can be depressing when you feel like everyone around you is lying or manipulating you for some reason or another."

Maddux smiled. "It's not all that different from the advertising industry then."

"No wonder you've been able to adjust so easily."

He glanced at her. "You've changed your tune about me. What did I do to make you think that?"

"You've been resourceful on this mission and refused to shy away from challenges."

"You mean like defying Pritchett and going after Voss?"

She nodded. "Pritchett will thank you later, that much you can be sure of."

"Unless Voss and Mikhailov are playing us right now."

"Now, you're really thinking like a spy."

"Or a skeptical conspiracy theorist."

"Maybe it'll be someone like you who solves the mystery behind Kennedy's death."

Maddux grimaced. "I'm afraid that case is open and shut. Lee Harvey Oswald handled that all by himself."

"I retract my earlier statement," she said, wagging her index finger. "You've still got some rough edges to smooth out before I deem you a dyed-in-the-wool spy."

"Why? Just because I think Oswald acted alone?"

She nodded. "Everyone knows there was another shooter—and it might have even been someone in our own agency."

"Well, no matter if you think I have a spy-worthy mind or not, I hope I've earned your trust on this operation."

"Haven't you been listening, Maddux? I don't trust anyone carte blanche, especially any man that turned down my advances."

"It's nothing personal, Barbara. But at this point in my life, I'm more concerned with the truth than I am with love."

"Does that apply to how you feel about Rose?"

Maddux shot her a sideways glance. He wasn't even certain if he wanted his relationship with Rose to go anywhere at all. In the few seconds he took to process the depth of Barbara's insulation, Maddux decided the best course of action was to remain silent.

He downshifted and the engine whined as he passed a car that he'd been behind for several minutes. Maddux returned the car back to its highest gear and stared only at the road that stretched out in front of him.

* * *

AFTER AN HOUR of driving in relative silence, Maddux pulled off the highway to get gas. He paid the attendant to fill up the tank before driving around to the side of the building.

"What are you doing?" Barbara asked.

"Otto was beat to hell. He needs to get out and stretch his legs."

"What if someone sees him and realizes that this car only has room for two passengers?"

"Do you see anyone around here?" Maddux asked, gesturing toward the field surrounding the small gas station.

She shook her head.

"It'll be fine." Maddux pushed a button that opened the compartment door, revealing a weary passenger. "How are things back there?"

"I'd almost rather return to prison," Voss said. "At least I have room to stretch out in there."

"I promise you that the food is much better with us and that you won't have to endure any torture sessions," Maddux said.

"I would laugh if it didn't hurt so much to do so."

Maddux smiled and offered his hand to Voss, helping him out of the cramped quarters and into the car. He wormed his way through, exiting on the passenger side as Barbara got out to make room for him.

"There's a restroom right there," Maddux said, pointing at a half-open door along the side of the gas station. "You might want to go in there and wash up."

"That'd be great," Voss said as he limped toward the building.

Maddux crossed his arms and leaned against the car, watching the sparse traffic speed by in the distance.

Barbara eased next to him. "Look, about what I said back there—"

"Don't worry about it. I'm just not sure I'm ready for anything in my personal life at this point. Other than this job, my focus is on finding out what happened to my father. I took my shot at love a long time ago, and I swung and missed."

"For what it's worth, I was married once too. So, I understand where you're coming from."

"Relationships just complicate everything. I'm trying to keep my life as simple as possible right now."

"I can respect that."

"But you don't feel the same way, do you?"

She sighed and shook her head.

"Truth be told, I'd rather be a normal woman, someone who's married and stays home with her kids. But that train left the station a long time ago."

"I'm sure there's still time if you want to make that happen."

She laughed softly. "I'm thirty-five years old, Maddux. I'm practically a spinster. Now, twenty years ago, there were plenty of unmarried women my age, mostly widowed by the war. But now? It's a challenge to find a woman my age who isn't married. At this age, I look like damaged goods."

"If there's one thing I learned about going through my divorce, it's that no matter how hard I wish I could go back in time and change the past, I must move forward with my life. I can't make the pain from my poor decisions go away, but I can resolve not to wallow in a pit of regret. I never thought my life would turn out the way it has, but here I am."

"And you don't want to take another shot at love?"

He shrugged. "Maybe one day, but that time isn't now."

The sound of a squeaky hinge swinging open arrested their attention. Voss stumbled out of the bathroom, his face absent of the mingled dirt and blood that had marred his appearance.

"Ready to go?" Maddux asked.

Voss shook his head. "I don't know if I'll ever be ready to climb back into a tight space like that."

"Fortunately, we only have two more hours before we get to the border," Barbara said. "We're supposed to have another car waiting for us once we reach a safe distance inside Germany."

"In that case, I can probably endure in there a little bit longer," Voss said.

Maddux and Barbara stood at the front of the car, serving as lookouts as Voss climbed in. Despite their extended stop, Maddux never saw another car or person on the premises.

"You ready to finish this thing?" Maddux asked.

Barbara nodded. "Just one more obstacle to go."

They rolled along for the next couple hours until they finally reached the border. The small guardhouse sat in the center of two lanes going in opposite directions. Aside from the two armed guards who roamed around without any apparent duties, the checkpoint seemed rather unimposing to Maddux.

However, the line of cars waiting to get into Germany stretched for more than a hundred meters.

"I've never seen this checkpoint so congested," Barbara said.

"What's it usually like?" Maddux asked.

"Three or four vehicles at the most."

Maddux glanced over his shoulder and scanned the area. A truck pulled up behind him, followed by a couple cars. After five minutes, the line still hadn't moved.

"I've got a bad feeling about this," Barbara said. "It usually takes no more than a minute or two to clear each car. And if there is something wrong, the drivers are typically instructed to pull over to the side where the armed guards conduct a more thorough inspection."

Maddux rolled his window down and leaned left, peering down the line toward the border exit.

"There doesn't appear to be any activity," he said. "I don't see any border agents standing next to any vehicles. It's almost like it's a ghost town."

"Maybe you should get out and see what's going on."

He shook his head. "I don't want to draw any more attention to us than necessary."

"Well, something is happening, and I don't like it."

Five more minutes dripped past before the sound of booming engines made Maddux and Barbara turn and look behind them.

"Well, this just got interesting," Maddux said as he watched an envoy of joint Russian and Czechoslovakian troop transports rumble along the line toward the checkpoint.

"I knew it," Barbara said before dropping her voice to a whisper. "We should've listened to Pritchett and left

Voss. It's like we're harboring Jonah, who's the reason for this storm."

"Maybe a giant fish will gobble us up and save us," Maddux quipped.

"This is not the time to make jokes," Barbara said.

"It's also not the time to panic."

Barbara remained focused on the troops milling around at the guardhouse. "We should've never let him go back to confront Mikhailov," she said. "I guarantee you this is why we have this sudden infusion of soldiers."

"You're probably right," Maddux said. "But we couldn't leave Voss there to die."

"We could have because he was the one making these ridiculous demands that you just went along with."

"I tried to put myself in his shoes."

Barbara set her jaw and narrowed her eyes. "We should've just left him right there."

"This isn't the time to cast blame either," Maddux said. "Rose built this car pretty tight. They're not going to find anything."

"How can you be so sure?"

"I trust Rose," he said. "I've seen what she can do. She's a miracle worker."

"Hopefully you're not being blinded by your affection for her."

Maddux glared at her. "Let's try to stay focused here—and calm. These soldiers will look at our papers and believe we're returning to Germany after being here on business. Let's not give them any reason to think otherwise."

Barbara nervously bounced her leg as the soldiers

fanned out, approaching cars and asking to see each traveler's papers.

Clamping his hand on Barbara's knee, Maddux looked at his partner. "Take a deep breath and relax."

Someone who appeared to be wearing an officer's uniform strolled along the road, peering inside random vehicles at will. When he arrived at their car, Maddux eased his hand off Barbara's twitching leg and took a deep breath.

"Good morning," Maddux said, forcing a smile. "Is there a problem at the border today?"

The man wore what seemed like a permanent scowl on his face. He glanced at his watch and held it up for Maddux to see.

"It's good afternoon," the man said. "Or in my case, a rather inconvenient one."

"Why is that?"

"We're looking for a person of interest."

"What did they do?" Maddux asked, steadying his voice.

"I am not at liberty to discuss it. But I assure you that this person will be caught. And he—along with anyone else who aided him in their attempted escape—will be dealt with severely."

"Good luck finding the man you're looking for," Maddux said.

The man stooped down to window level and scoped out the inside for a few tense seconds before standing.

"We will return shortly," the man said.

Maddux rolled up his window and looked at Barbara.

"Was that him?" he asked.

"Who?"

"Mikhailov."

A tapping sound came from the hidden compartment. However, Maddux refused to open it up for fear that a guard would see and Voss would be discovered. Yet the rat-a-tat-tat persisted.

"What is it?" Maddux asked, slightly raising his voice.

"That was him," Voss said, his voice muffled by the thick padded wall.

"Mikhailov?" Barbara asked.

"Yes."

"Are you sure?" Maddux asked.

"I hear that man's voice in my sleep," Voss answered.

"Now what?" Barbara asked. "I'm sure he's coming back for a second look."

"Are all our papers in order?"

She nodded and retrieved them from the glove box. Maddux took the papers and flipped through them to make sure everything looked correct.

"I want to make sure we make this go as smooth as possible on our end."

Barbara sifted through a few more items in the compartment.

"What are these for?" she asked, holding up a pair of gloves.

"Be very careful with those," Maddux said. "They're for use only in an emergency situation."

"What kind of emergency?"

"Why don't you hand them to me right now?" he said. "I think this might qualify as the kind of emergency Rose referred to."

A few moments later, a soldier knocked on their window and held out his hand. Maddux rolled his window down.

"Papers, please," the soldier demanded.

Maddux furnished the man with the requested visas and passports while remaining silent.

"Were you here for business or pleasure?" the soldier asked.

"Business," Maddux asked.

The soldier crouched down and looked at Barbara in the passenger side. He broke into a wide grin.

"Are you sure it wasn't pleasure?" he said with a wink.

"No, it was all business," Maddux answered.

The soldier nodded and scanned the paper. "I guess I'll have to take your word for it."

Collecting the papers, the soldier stacked them orderly again, using the car's roof to do so. He handed them back to Maddux and then opened the driver's side door.

"I'm going to need you to step out."

Maddux eyed the soldier closely. "What for? Is there something wrong?"

"We must thoroughly inspect all vehicles. It's just protocol."

"I don't see you doing that to every other car," Barbara said, her voice tinged with angst. "Is it because we're Americans?"

The soldier glared at her.

"It is because you are here at this gate while someone is trying to escape our country who deserves to be punished—and punished severely."

A pair of soldiers hustled over to Maddux's vehicle and began rifling through it. They pulled out all their luggage, unapologetically tossing clothes and toiletries onto the ground. When they were finished, the soldiers stuffed the contents back inside and zipped it up.

"Are we clear to leave now?" Maddux asked when it appeared the search had ended.

The soldier in charge shook his head.

"Please return to your vehicle and drive it over there," he said, pointing to a lane that was marked off by traffic cones.

Maddux followed the soldier's orders and stepped out of the car again. Barbara did likewise, joining him near the trunk. They both watched as Mikhailov stormed toward them.

"What are we gonna do about him?" Barbara said.

"Remember those gloves?" Maddux said as he fished them out of his pocket and pulled them snug on his hands.

"What do they do?"

"You'll find out soon enough."

When Mikhailov reached them, he circled the car once more.

"Are we free to go now?" Maddux asked. "I think it's evident that we don't have any stowaways."

Mikhailov narrowed his eyes and set his jaw. "You'll leave when I say you can leave," he said with a growl. "Now step back."

He opened the trunk and tossed the two suitcases onto the ground again. Maddux's zipper broke upon impact, resulting in his clothes strewn all around them. A team of four soldiers joined Mikhailov and used mirrors to look beneath the car.

Mikhailov stuck his head inside the trunk and began knocking against the sides. Maddux and Barbara glanced at each other, both holding their breath.

Mikhailov stood upright and crossed his arms. He motioned with his index finger at Maddux, summoning him closer.

"I need you to answer some questions for me," the StB officer asked. Mikhailov looked inside the trunk again and then back at Maddux. "Where were you last night?"

"At our hotel, sir," Maddux said.

"Then how come a car with this exact description was reportedly seen leaving an StB facility early this morning?" Mikhailov asked.

"What time was it?" Maddux asked.

"Around six-thirty."

"While it was still dark?"

Mikhailov pursed his lips and scowled. "What are you trying to imply?"

"I was awake at that time getting ready for our trip home—and it was still dark outside," Maddux said. "Perhaps someone made a mistake in reporting what they saw."

Mikhailov eyed Maddux closely before taking one final peek inside the trunk and knocking on the walls.

"I'll be watching you," Mikhailov said. "The next time you request to come into my country, I'll make sure you don't sneeze without someone being there to make a note of it. And, Mr. Maddux?"

"Yes."

"I never forget a face."

Maddux held out his hand to shake the disgruntled StB officer's, who reluctantly obliged.

"I look forward to it," Maddux said. "Though it will be a waste of your resources." Then with a whisper, "I hear there are far more nefarious agents already hiding inside your own borders."

"Get out," Mikhailov bellowed. "And don't let me ever see you in this country again."

Maddux and Barbara returned to their vehicle. Carefully removing his gloves, Maddux dropped them into a bag and cinched it shut before the two agents proceeded toward the gate.

XXV

MADDUX FOLLOWED THE DIRECTIONS of the soldier standing at the end of the lane as he directed them back to the main road out of Czechoslovakia. The guard at the gatehouse asked for their papers before stamping and returning them.

"I hope you enjoyed your visit," the guard said.

"It was interesting," Maddux said. He handed the papers to Barbara for safe keeping before rolling up the window and driving through the neutral zone.

"That went over well," Barbara said.

Maddux glanced nervously at the mirror.

"What are you worried about now?" she asked.

"I'm just hoping he doesn't drop dead before we get out of sight," he said.

"Drop dead? What did you do?"

"Those gloves were a gift from Rose—and they were laced with poison. Once he shook my hand, he sealed his own fate. So, just be careful while handling those things. It's probably best for us to dispose of that bag the moment we stop."

"I'll remind you," she said with a sigh.

Maddux rolled up to the German border gatehouse and presented his papers. The guard didn't look at them for more than thirty seconds before stamping the documents and waving Maddux through.

"Should we tell Otto what you just did?" Barbara asked.

"Not yet," Maddux said. "Besides, he should probably just get the news as a pleasant surprise once it's confirmed. I trust Rose, but I'm sure there was some kind of margin for error with those things. I don't know how long it takes for them to work, though she assured me they were fast."

"I'm not up on my poisons, though I should be. It's sometimes the best way to discreetly remove someone."

"*Remove?* Is that what the agency is calling it these days?" he said with a chuckle.

"I don't care what word you use for it as long as the threat is eliminated."

"Well, Mikhailov would've continued to threaten us, not to mention Otto if something wasn't done about it. His inability to let things go just led to his demise."

After a half hour, Maddux reached the spot where a car had been left for them. He considered how uncomfortable Voss must have been during the ride, unaware of the tense drama unfolding around him. Maddux and Barbara helped their passenger out of the hidden compartment. After being stuffed into such tight quarters for so long, Voss asked for more time to stretch and walk around. Once he felt he was somewhat back to normal and all feeling had returned to his extremities, he notified Maddux and they got into the car together, while Barbara took the extra vehicle.

"Thanks for letting me drive back with Otto," Maddux said. "We have much to discuss."

Barbara gave Maddux a kiss on his cheek. "You're a good partner," Barbara said. "And an even better agent."

"You need to stop heaping all this praise on me or else I'll get the big head," he said.

"Sadly, there's nothing I can do about that. Your head is already huge," she added with a wink.

Maddux returned to his car where Voss was waiting.

"She likes you, you know?" Voss said.

Maddux shrugged, hoping to avoid the topic for the rest of the ride back to Bonn. "Maybe she does; maybe she doesn't. It's hard to tell with women sometimes."

Voss shook his head. "No, it's easy to tell. She definitely likes you. And she's quite attractive too."

Maddux smiled and wagged his index finger. "Careful, Otto. I might have to tell Ingrid what you said."

Voss let out a hearty laugh. "Ingrid knows that she's the only woman for me. If something happened, she knows that no one else would ever take me."

"Don't sell yourself short," Maddux said. "You're sharp and intelligent—and you have most of your hair."

"What I do have is gray though," he said with a sigh.

"Well, I guess you can't have it all, now can you?"

"Guess not. That's what happens when you've been around as long as I have."

"Long enough to meet my father?"

Voss stopped and stared at Maddux before returning a pensive gaze to the highway. "I did promise you that I'd tell you about him, didn't I?"

Maddux nodded.

"Well," Voss began, "the man that I think is your

father was named John Hambrick and worked one summer with me at a Russian institute outside Moscow."

"My father was working with the Russians?" Maddux asked.

"That's how it appeared on the surface, though I doubt he really was. It was difficult to trust anyone at that facility. I held everyone at arm's length, though I can say that I was approached by both European and Russian allies alike to report on the other side's activities."

"But it was a research facility?"

"Yes, there was a great deal of suspicion that existed between the scientists from various countries. Some of the scientists sent there were nothing of the sort. They were undoubtedly spies first with a minimal understanding and knowledge of the field in which they were dealing with."

"And the others?"

"There were a handful of men who were obviously scientists first, as their espionage skills were seriously lacking. They would say the most ridiculous thing that tipped everyone off what their secondary purpose for attending was."

"What about my father? Where did he fit in?"

"To be honest, I'm not sure if he was a spy, which probably means if he was, he was a good one."

"Did you get the opportunity to interact with him much?"

"Not really. He was on campus with the rest of us, but he didn't seem too interested in making friends. If anything, he went out of his way to make it obvious that he was there for the job and the job only."

"Hmm," Maddux said, staring distantly at the road.

"What is it?"

"Well, that just doesn't sound like him. He loved his work, but he was always spending time with his friends or brothers. The number of weekends when we didn't go over to someone else's house or host one of his friends or family members were few and far between. My father was the kind of man who left his work at the office and was fully present when he walked in the door."

"Sounds like a good father."

Maddux sighed and shook his head. "Not if he ditched our family, including his wife, to be a spy."

Voss shifted in his seat and turned to face Maddux. "I would be careful about jumping to any conclusions regarding his motives," Voss said. "Perhaps he felt like he was doing the right thing. Noble men often make great sacrifices."

"Sacrifices at the expense of your family seem too steep a price," Maddux said.

"So, your opinion of your father has changed since you believe that he voluntarily entered the CIA?"

Maddux nodded. "I used to think of him as my hero when I was a young boy. Then when I was told that he jumped off the Brooklyn Bridge and killed himself, I thought of him as a coward. But when I heard that he might be alive, I can't tell you all the emotions I felt—anger, bitterness, disappointment. Honestly, I can't seem to straighten them all out."

"Well, I'm no counselor, but I do know that from what I knew of your father—if that was indeed him—he was a kind and generous man. He treated everyone with respect and often acted in deference to his colleagues, even when he was right. And let me tell you, that's not typical behavior among elite and well-accomplished scientists like the ones who were in Moscow that summer."

"Where did everyone go when it ended?"

"They went back to their normal research institutes, all of us carting home stacks of useful information that we gathered during collaboration. Everything I learned was as if I had crammed five years of learning and testing into about four months."

"And you don't know where my father went?"

Voss shook his head. "There was a directory published that listed contact information for all of the scientists who participated, but I didn't work as closely with your father as some of the others."

"Do you still have that directory?"

"If I did, it'd be at my former office in Prague, but I doubt it. I purge quite often, especially things that I don't use enough to deem important to keep. I'm sure that directory would've fallen into that category."

"Do you at least remember what country he was working for?"

"He was definitely working for the Russians."

"How can you be sure?"

"It wasn't uncommon to see American and British scientists working for Russia. They pay their scientists very well, especially those who are assisting in government-related activities. If you can stomach working for a regime determined to dominate the world through incendiary tactics, it's easily one of the best jobs available in our profession."

Maddux glanced at his passenger. "What changed your mind?"

"I simply want to be a scientist, to study this incredible world we live in. But Mikhailov and other StB officials seemed intent on making me a spy. I've never met a single colleague who wished he was a spy. We're all fascinated by how things work and are driven by the desire to study them and create new ways to harness them to make the world a better place. I never once considered that someone might force me to use my knowledge to create weapons."

"Wasn't that what you were doing in the U.S., too?"

Voss nodded. "I can't say I'm proud of everything I've done in the name of science. Working for the Nazis is the thing I'm least proud of, but it was a matter of survival. It's easy to look back and condemn my time working under their direction, but if I hadn't, they would've gassed me and my family."

"I'm not interested in judging you. It'd be nice if the world was truly black and white, but it's more like a million shades of gray."

"Thank you for believing in me," Voss said. "I must say that the burden of what I carry around is unbearable at times. The things I've seen, the things I've done—it terrifies me."

"You're not alone there either. But we do the best we can to protect the people we love."

Voss laughed softly.

"What is it?" Maddux asked.

"You remind me of your father," Voss said. "He was so kind and compassionate. He'd be proud of the man you've become."

"Perhaps. There's much more beneath the surface that you don't see."

"What's underneath pushes the best to the top—and that's what I think about you. You came back for me when you didn't need to. And I'll be forever grateful."

"No thanks necessary," Maddux said. "You deserve to have someone extend some trust to you for once in your life."

"I hope your decision pays off for you."

Maddux smiled. "It already has."

THE NEXT MORNING, Maddux snuck Voss into the CIA station for a debriefing with Pritchett. However, that meeting was put on hold when Pritchett saw Voss and directed him to the medical ward to be examined. After a half hour, the doctor released Voss with some aspirin and a few bandages, including a splint on his pinky finger.

When they reconvened for the meeting in the conference room, Barbara joined them.

"So, would I hate to see the other guy?" Pritchett asked with a slight smile.

Voss shook his head. "The coward who did this to me never gave me a chance to fight back."

Pritchett adjusted the patch over his eye and then pushed a file folder across the table to Voss. "The coward who did this to you is dead."

Voss opened the folder to read a cable from the Prague station chief. "Dead? How?"

"You can thank the man on your left," Pritchett said, glancing at Maddux.

Mouth gaping, Voss looked at Maddux. "How did— you didn't—?"

"I didn't tell you because I didn't know if worked," Maddux said.

"What worked?"

"The poison glove I shook Mikhailov's hand with yesterday."

"A poison glove killed him? Where do you find such things?"

Pritchett laughed. "Let's just say we have a secret weapon here at our facility who works magic."

"It's *science*," Maddux corrected. "Don't ever suggest to Rose that what she does is magic. It's not pretty."

A wide grin swept across Voss's face. He slapped the table and stood before pumping his fists. "I'm free," Voss said. "I can't believe it. I'm truly free."

Pritchett turned somber and used his hook to point at Voss's seat, gesturing for him to sit down. "I'm afraid there's something I need to tell you."

Voss eased into his chair and leaned forward, his eyes wide. "Please tell me Ingrid and Astrid are okay— please."

"I wish I could, but the truth is we don't know," Pritchett said.

"What do you mean, you *don't know*?"

"I don't know how else to break this to you, Dr. Voss, but your wife is a spy for the KGB."

Voss leaned back in his chair and wrinkled his face. "That's absurd. I think I would know if my wife was a spy. She went along with me and . . ."

Voss stopped and covered his mouth, a revelation apparently dawning upon him.

"How could I have been so blind?" he mumbled as he removed his hand from his mouth.

Maddux patted Voss on the back. "I think I can say this in all honesty—I know how you feel."

Voss mouthed a *thank you* to Maddux before turning to Pritchett. "But how did you find this out? And where is Astrid?"

"Ironically enough, we learned it from the bugs you planted," Pritchett began. "Our agents in Prague heard a discussion about a spy in the United States, one that had infiltrated the science community with her husband through faking a defection. It didn't take us long to figure out who that was."

"Ingrid!" Voss said through clenched teeth.

"But I'm afraid there's more."

"Go on," Voss said, burying his head in his hands.

"Apparently, your wife had planted a bug on you and the KGB was able to learn about the location of a secret research facility in the Alps, one where the allies are working together to develop technologies to destabilize the Russian's new missile defense program."

"The anti-ballistic missile system?" Voss asked.

"That's the one. From what we know about it right now, Moscow would be a difficult city to attack in the event of a nuclear weapons launch. And so a group of allied scientists are collaborating to figure out a solution."

"You want to attack Moscow?"

Pritchett shook his head. "That's not the plan right now, but we need to be ready in case we're forced to do so. However, that's only half of the problem. Your wife is more than just a spy—she's a fully-trained KGB operative, and she's going to launch an attack on the facility in two days."

"Ingrid is going to attack a facility?" Voss asked.

"I know this might be hard for you to fathom, but it's apparent from the communiqués we intercepted that she's a valuable KGB asset," Pritchett said. "She's likely been spying on some of your colleagues in Prague to make sure that no one was getting out of line or sharing secrets and research with the allies."

Voss sighed. "It's starting to make sense now."

"What do you mean?" Maddux asked.

"I've had several fellow scientists go missing after expressing their desire to leave the country," Voss said. "They would complain to me one day and then they'd be gone. I used to think the facility was bugged."

"It probably was," Barbara said.

"Yes, but some of these conversations happened when we were walking home or at a private dinner party," Voss said. "I know that several times these colleagues were confiding in me. No one else heard what they said."

"Except you told your wife, didn't you?" Pritchett said.

Voss nodded. "I remember one of the men who expressed his desire to return to seek refuge in Germany was suddenly reassigned, the very day after he'd told me that he wanted to leave. Now, I know it had to be because I told Ingrid."

Pritchett leaned back in his seat and sipped his coffee before speaking. "I'm very sorry about breaking this news to you in this way," Pritchett said. "The truth is the CIA suspected that there was a breach in the facility you

were working at in New York. We had struggled to identify the mole and actually thought it was you when you
hopped on a plane and tried to sneak back into Czechoslovakia. But it's now apparent we were looking in the
wrong place."

"How could I have let this happen? What is to become of me—and Astrid? What about her?"

"We are still working hard to locate your daughter,"
Pritchett said. "Our initial intelligence report suggests
that Ingrid might be using your daughter as a way to navigate difficult roadblocks in her attempt to attack the facility. While using a child isn't unprecedented, it is rare
and most agents aren't inclined to give a mother traveling
with her daughter a second look."

"So, people are going to die because of what I've
done?" Voss asked.

"You've done nothing wrong," Pritchett said.
"You've simply been the target of a well-crafted plot or-
chestrated by a devious government that has no regard
for a child's well-being. To use your daughter as a pawn
is despicable. But I can assure you that we will do everything to find her, keep her safe, and return her to you."

"And what will become of Ingrid?"

"That depends on when we find her and what that
situation is like—if we find her at all."

"I've done more harm than good, as always," Voss
said, his voice forlorn.

Pritchett shook his head. "I'm afraid that's just not
true, Dr. Voss. Not only did we uncover the source of
the leak in our facility in New York—"

"One I put there," Voss interrupted.

"If it hadn't been you, it would've been someone

else. But your cooperation here helped us figure out what was happening. You also helped us discover something else that was happening in Prague, right under your nose."

"And what was that?"

"Former Nazi scientist Ernst Duerr was working in an underground facility in the city that was developing a more accurate long-range missile, one that could be equipped to carry nuclear warheads."

"And what has become of it?"

"A gas leak led to its destruction—at least, that's the official report the government has given the media. However, we happen to know who helped create this gas leak."

"And what about Duerr?"

"We believe he died in the explosion along with several other scientists, though none of that has been confirmed yet, either by us or by government officials."

"So what happens next?" Maddux asked.

Pritchett looked at Maddux and then glanced at Barbara. "It just so happens that Opel has a manufacturing plant near the facility Ingrid is planning to attack," Pritchett said. "And apparently, you two need to go visit it this week."

"You want us to stop the attack?" Maddux asked.

"I couldn't think of any tandem more suited for the task than you two, especially the way you managed to outwit the StB and escape without ever drawing an inkling of suspicion that you had anything to do with Voss's escape."

"You aren't upset about us going back and retrieving Voss against your orders?" Maddux asked.

"We'll discuss that at a different time," Pritchett said. "For now, we must put all of our energies into stopping Ingrid. If she manages to somehow succeed, the whole world may suffer."

"Why not send troops in to protect the building since it's obvious the Russians now know its location?" Barbara asked.

"Unfortunately, it can't be moved or fortified in such a short period of time," Pritchett said. "It's not even supposed to be there according to our several peace-time treaties that the U.S. and her allies have signed."

"But if the Russians expose it?"

"If they tell the world that they know we have a facility there, they'll be exposing themselves as breaking a treaty, giving them no ground to stand on. But if an explosion occurs in the mountains and government entities investigate, they get away with continuing to spy as well as currying political favor. They'd look innocent and justified in rebuking the allies for breaking terms of the treaty. Meanwhile, the allies would look sheepishly guilty. But we're not going to let that happen, are we?"

"You can count on us," Maddux said.

"Good," Pritchett said. "Go pack your bags. This mission will be the most important one you've been on yet."

XXVII

LATER THAT AFTERNOON, Maddux descended into the bowels of the CIA's offices to visit Rose Fuller. The trip to see her was strictly business—at least, that's what he told himself. He peered into the stainless steel door of the elevator before it opened to make sure his hair was combed neatly in place.

"You made it back in one piece," Rose said, her face lighting up as soon as she noticed Maddux.

"Were you doubting that I would?"

She shrugged. "Sometimes the tech doesn't quite pan out."

"Define *sometimes*."

"Oh, let's not get into statistics right now. I'm just happy to see you came back in one piece. Apparently, the car worked out great for you."

"It was quite functional. But this time, I was hoping for something a little more flashy."

She put her hands on her hips and eyed him cautiously. "And what exactly did you have in mind?

"I was thinking that the Ferrari Dino 206 GT over there looks mighty lonely and needs to be taken out for a spin."

"That's funny," she said. "I hadn't heard her complain at all about being lonely."

"Perhaps you don't speak her language."

Rose winked at Maddux and walked across the room. She stopped in front of an open metal box hanging on the wall and selected a key. Upon returning to Maddux, she tossed the key to him. "I guess it wouldn't hurt to let you drive her on this mission," she said. "I hear that you have a lengthy drive ahead of you."

"The operation takes place near Füssen on Lake Alpsee."

"Rather an interesting place to put a secret lab for the allies, don't you think?"

"I can't waste any more mental energy trying to figure out why things are done the way they are around here," Maddux said. "All I know is that they simply are— and I must deal with what I know."

"Maybe you'd be more speculative over dinner and a glass of wine."

Maddux smiled and shook his head. "If I didn't know any better, I'd think that was a come-on line."

"You're the spy trained to discern messages from friend and foe alike. You're free to interpret it how you wish."

"Am I really?"

Rose turned coyly toward the table with gadgets spread across it. "Pritchett gave me a brief rundown on your mission yesterday, so I came up with a few items I think you might find useful."

"The shoes worked well, by the way. In fact, they probably saved my life."

Rose chuckled. "That's the same thing I say whenever I find a pair of comfortable shoes."

"Well, it's not hyperbole in my case."

"It's not hyperbole either when I say this watch might save your life too," Rose said, holding up the timepiece by the leather band.

"How does it work?" Maddux asked as he moved closer to the table.

"You simply hit the latch forcefully with the back of your other wrist, setting off the device, like so," Rose said, slipping it on and giving a demonstration.

The moment she knocked the watch's latch against her wrist, a plume of smoke exploded into the air, temporarily disorienting Maddux.

"What was that?" he asked.

"Should I dare say *magic*?" she said with a laugh. "Don't worry about how it works, just know that it does."

She handed Maddux an identical watch.

"Just beware that this watch is a one-time use," she said. "I'm working on getting multiple bursts of blinding smoke, but this will have to suffice in the interim."

"Fantastic," Maddux said. "Anything else you think might come in handy?"

"Here's a pen you could use as a type of grenade," she said. "Just click it once and then you have three seconds before it explodes, sending shards of the pen in every direction. It's not necessarily a life-saver, but it will buy you some time if you're in a pinch."

Rose placed the pen in Maddux's hand. "Just be careful not to sign anything with this pen, okay?"

"Sure thing," Maddux said, sliding the device into his front breast pocket. "Anything else?"

"I think that covers it," she said. "The car has plenty

of features, but I have a feeling you're more interested in how it looks than all the bells and whistles I added to it."

"Are you sure you're not the field operative with a keen sense of intuition like that?"

Rose laughed and waved dismissively. "Good luck," she said. "I'll be anxious to hear how everything worked upon your return."

* * *

EARLY THE NEXT MORNING, Maddux met Barbara at the CIA offices before heading south to Füssen. He climbed into the car and then glanced at the watch Rose had given him, while waiting for Barbara to get in. He straightened his tie before inserting the key and twisting it. The roar of the Ferrari echoed in garage.

Barbara flung open the door and slid into her seat.

"This is a far nicer ride than our last trip," she said, running her hands along the leather seats.

"It's far faster too," Maddux said before he released the clutch and stomped on the accelerator.

The car lurched forward, the tires squealing as he exited the garage and drove out through the parking deck. Maddux emerged onto the street and put on a pair of sunglasses to help dull the bright morning sunshine.

"So, was it worth it?" she asked after they exited the city.

"Was what worth it?"

"Saving Otto Voss? Did he tell you what you hoped you'd hear?"

"In some ways it was."

"Such as?"

"It made me feel closer to my father. Voss's stories

about him helped me get a better sense of who my father is—or was."

"But it didn't get you any closer to finding him, did it?"

Maddux shook his head. "Unfortunately, it raised more questions than answers."

"Think he was playing on your sympathies?"

"No, Voss is genuine. Ambivalent, maybe, as well as naïve from time to time. But definitely authentic. He doesn't have a manipulative bone in his body."

"You do realize this could all be a big set up, right?"

Maddux rubbed the side of his face and gazed at the rolling hills as the Ferrari hummed along. "Are you this distrusting of everyone?"

"Stick with this business long enough, and you'll join me in my cynicism."

"At some point, you have to trust another person, Barbara. Not everyone is trying to get something from you all the time."

"The moment you let your guard down is the moment you get taken."

"That doesn't sound like an axiom I'd find in a fortune cookie," Maddux said. "People are far more complicated than that."

"Doesn't mean I'm not right."

"Doesn't mean that you are either."

"Look, Maddux, if you want to go on living in la-la land where everything is perfect and everybody means exactly what they say, be my guest. Just know that fairytale land and the real world of espionage cannot coexist."

"Sounds like you think there's a big bad wolf just around every bend."

"That's because there is."

Maddux drove on for another hour without saying a word. He let Barbara handle the radio duties, ensuring that they listened to good music sung in English for the majority of their trip. Finally, he interrupted a Buddy Holly song by turning off the radio.

"What are you doing?" she asked.

"We've heard that one twice already on this trip. It's grating on me."

"I love that song," she said as she reached to turn the radio back on.

"I dated a Peggy Sue one time. She shattered my heart into a thousand pieces. I'd rather not listen to it again."

Barbara drew back and shot him a sideways glance. "Still painful, huh?"

Maddux nodded.

"Well, I knew an Elvis once who led me on before he ditched me. I can't listen to any of Elvis's songs either."

"Don't say that in public," Maddux said. "You might get attacked for speaking out against The King."

"Speaking of attacks, we need to go over our plan for tomorrow," she said.

"What exactly did Pritchett ask you to do?"

"He wants me to evacuate everyone in the facility without Ingrid seeing so she doesn't become suspicious that something else is going on."

"You think her mission is about killing scientists or destroying the lab?"

"Her foremost objective will be to raze the lab and all the research that's inside," Barbara said. "But I'm sure she wouldn't lose any sleep over killing a few scientists either."

"Is there a way out?"

"There is an emergency passageway to escape from that comes out on the other side of the mountain. It goes way back into the mountain. I'm going to have three busses parked there, all driven by CIA agents stationed in Austria. They will be posing as tour guides. We should have enough space to get everyone onto those three busses."

"And then what?"

"You make sure that the place is safe, disarming all the weapons."

"If it's just Ingrid, I doubt she's going to be carrying many explosives," Maddux said. "One well-placed device should do the trick."

"I wouldn't be so sure. You're going to need to do a thorough check."

"I'll be thorough. Don't worry."

"This isn't going to be like some of those drills you run in training," she said. "Active weapons in a live situation aren't the same as simulations. You'll need to have nerves of steel and quick thinking if you're going to get out of this alive."

Maddux glanced over at her. "Do you think I'm capable of this?"

She nodded. "You've proven to me that you're more than competent, but I want you to know what you're walking into. Ingrid may look sweet on the outside. However, if she's a highly-trained KGB operative like Pritchett said, she'll be a devil on the inside and you'll have one hell of a time stopping her."

Maddux winked at her. "I'm looking forward to the challenge."

"Good because you're going to have your hands full with her."

XXVIII

EARLY THE NEXT MORNING, Maddux and Barbara parted ways at the chalet they stayed at in Füssen. Maddux watched her get onto a tour bus driven by a fellow CIA agent from Austria and disappear around the bend. With the cool nip in the air, Maddux got behind the wheel of his car and headed toward the secret lab nestled in the side of a mountain overlooking Lake Alpsee.

When Maddux roared around the corner revealing a pristine body of water, he couldn't help but admire the natural beauty engulfing the area. Jagged mountain peaks extended just beyond the towering pines that covered the landscape. The lake was small by most standards with less than a couple miles of shoreline. But what it lacked in size, it made up for with its rich-blue hue and surrounding majestic cliffs. The pair of German castles, Hohenschwangau and Neuschwanstein, soared in the distance like a pair of crown jewels.

And these scientists are in a lab all day long with this beauty all around them?

Maddux couldn't fathom such a cruel fate, though

he had to admit the lab's location was genius. Most secret facilities he'd read about existed in barren wildernesses. Remaining indoors—and hidden—would be much easier in a desert location rather than just minutes away from some of Europe's most visited castles, he presumed.

Who would ever go looking here?

The Russians hadn't. They stumbled on the lab's location due to asset placement and a bit of luck rather than sheer espionage. According to Pritchett's report, the lab's location was never to be spoken of and only a handful of people in New York even knew of its existence. But one of those people had said something they shouldn't have—and Ingrid pinpointed the facility. And if all the CIA's intel was correct, she was going to destroy the research lab too.

Due to the secretive nature of the facility—and its positioning deep inside the mountain—access would be tricky, even for someone who knew the place even existed. However, destroying it wouldn't actually necessitate breaking inside. A well-placed weapon on the outside would suffice.

Maddux checked his watch. At just a shade before 8:00 a.m., he took up a position on a nearby cliff overlooking the facility's entrance. The protocol for getting into the building was rather tedious. Employees would go through a mountain tunnel that had a lane that appeared to lead to nowhere but a brick wall. However, a guard monitoring the gate granted access while watching on a closed-circuit monitor. Once inside, the guard would then check credentials before releasing a series of blockades to allow the person through. A parking deck was located at the bottom of the winding road down through the mountain, and a guarded entrance was located there as well.

Maddux peered through his binoculars into the access tunnel where a large box truck approached the entrance to the facility parking lot at a high rate of speed. He watched as the driver bailed out at the last minute and the truck rammed into the door. Maddux saw a couple guards run after the man, returning fire as he shot at them. He finally toppled to the ground, apparently dead. But his mission was accomplished—the door wasn't going to be easily opened.

Maddux looked on top of the ridge, searching for a sign that Barbara had evacuated the employees. But there was none. She was supposed to signal once everyone was safely removed. All he could see in the distance were empty tour busses awaiting passengers. Moments later, he heard an explosion.

What the—?

He looked back toward the direction of the secret passageway and saw smoke rising.

What had happened was clear to Maddux. The intel the CIA received said nothing about Ingrid working with other operatives. But there was no denying it now. Maddux doubted the man who was driving the truck had set an explosive elsewhere, so that meant at least three KGB agents were involved in orchestrating the attack.

And still no sign of Ingrid.

Maddux redirected his attention to the cliff, figuring the bomb was most likely planted there. As he scanned slowly across the rock face, he noticed hundreds of nooks and crannies in which to place an explosive. After five minutes, his frustration level almost hit a boiling point until he noticed a glint off a silver object tucked about halfway up the mountainside just above a ledge measuring about five square meters.

He zoomed in closer on the object, and it looked more like an explosive device than before.

That's got to be it.

Maddux looked back toward the extraction point for Barbara and the other lab workers. Smoke plumes billowed from the site, but still no sign of any people.

Tucking his binoculars into his pack, he cinched it and slung it over his shoulders before racing toward the rock wall. The most worrisome part for Maddux was the fact that he didn't know how much time remained before the bomb exploded—not to mention that all the scientists were likely still trapped inside.

It took him several minutes to make his way to the rock wall and stare upward.

Why does everything always have to be in the air? Could it be on the ground just once?

He dug his heels into the rock and worked his way upward, climbing about ten meters up before he reached the ledge. Pulling himself on top, he scrambled over to the device. Maddux removed his backpack and set it down next to him. The clock display counted down, clicking past five minutes as he picked the bomb up. Before he could make another move, he felt a gun barrel forced into the back of his head.

"Hands up, and move slowly," a woman said.

Maddux complied, easing his hands into the air and cautiously turning around. The gun was inches from his forehead. The woman flashed a wry grin.

"Don't even think about it," she said.

"You must be Ingrid Voss," Maddux said.

"And you must be CIA," she said. "It's a pity you attempted to stop me today."

"If you're going to shoot me, just get it over with."

She shook her head. "No, you're too valuable to me. How else do you think I'm going to get my husband back?"

"You think he wants to come back to you?"

"My husband is the most loyal man on Earth."

"And you've betrayed his trust. He had no idea you were a spy."

"Is that what he told you? That man is brilliant, I swear."

Maddux eyed her closely, cocking his head to one side. "I don't believe you."

She chuckled. "I'm not asking you to believe me. I honestly couldn't care less about what you think. But I am going to use you to get my husband back. The CIA will gladly make an exchange for one of their agents. They do it all the time."

Maddux glanced at the clock, which showed less than four minutes remaining.

"Now, let's move," she said. "I don't want to end my life on this stupid rock."

Maddux shrugged. "Lead the way. I don't know where I'm going."

Using her foot, she shoved Maddux in the back, sending him stumbling forward. Instead of using his hands to catch himself, he brought them behind his head and slapped his watch against his wrist. A blast of white powder flew into Ingrid's face.

Wasting no time, Maddux dropped to the ground and swept Ingrid's leg from beneath her. She hit the ground hard but rolled away from him. She tucked her gun in her pants and lunged toward Maddux. With some of the powder still lingering in the air, she hit him just above his knees, toppling him. They both rolled over several times, each one trying to gain an advantage and wind up on top.

But neither one could gain the upper hand, resulting in them trading punches and grabbing each other's arms as they lay side by side. The struggle lasted less than thirty seconds before Ingrid decided to go for her gun. And when she did, Maddux was prepared.

He punched her hard in the shoulder, knocking her gun loose as they both made a mad dash for the weapon. But in the scramble to grab it, the gun tumbled over the ledge and down the mountain, discharging once before falling to rest ten meters below.

Maddux grabbed her by her shirt and pulled her toward him. He scrambled over near the bomb before he stooped down to search for a weapon in his backpack. Cocking the gun, he held it to her head.

"It's over, Ingrid," he said. "You lost."

"What are you going to do? Shoot me right here? You're orphaning a little girl if you do."

Maddux glared at her. "Where's Astrid?"

"I'm certainly not going to tell you where she is if that gun is pointed at me." She glanced at the clock. "Actually, you better decide what's more important to you: capturing me or dismantling the bomb and saving all those people trapped inside—because you do not have time to do both. I am willing to die for what I believe in. Are you?"

Maddux growled in frustration.

"Just think about all those innocent people," she said.

Maddux exhaled and turned his attention to the bomb. While he knew Ingrid didn't care about the people inside, she was right. He couldn't let them die.

Maddux glanced over his shoulder at the ledge. Ingrid was already gone. Just a few seconds into trying to figure out how to disarm the bomb, Maddux realized he didn't have enough time.

He placed the bomb in his pack and started to climb down the rock face. As he did, his hands started to sweat and he could feel himself slipping. His left hand suddenly gave way, leaving him swinging back and forth from a grip that was no more than a half-inch long.

Taking a deep breath and summoning all of his strength, he used his right arm to swing himself over to another handhold. He dug his feet into the rocks and continued climbing down until he reached the bottom.

Then he did the only thing he could do—run.

XXIX

MADDUX PUMPED HIS ARMS and reached farther with each stride. Lake Alpsee loomed ahead about 400 meters, but it seemed like five miles to him under the circumstances. Ever since he made the decision to get rid of the bomb, he started counting in his head. If his internal clock was aligned with the one ticking in his backpack, he calculated he had ninety seconds remaining.

Eighty-nine, eighty-eight . . .

With each step, his muscles burned as if his entire body might spontaneously combust.

Keep moving.

Up ahead, Lake Alpsee sat serene nestled among the rising landscape of the Bavarian Alps. However, several couples walked hand-in-hand along the bank. And given that Maddux had no idea just how big of a blast the bomb would make, he became concerned.

"Get off the shore!" he yelled. "Get off the shore!"

The couples stared at him, unable to move. Maddux imagined they must've thought he escaped from an asylum. Then he wondered if they even spoke English.

In the rush of the moment, he couldn't translate the phrase into Germany.

"*Achtung! Achtung!*" was all he could muster.

The couples dispersed, one running to his left, the other to his right.

Fifteen, fourteen, thirteen . . .

Maddux pulled his pack in front of him as he ran and dug out the bomb. He tossed the pack to the side and hit the shoreline. Then he flung the explosive as high and far as he could.

Four, three, two, one . . .

A guttural-sounding explosion shook the banks a brief second before a column of water raced skyward, resulting in wide-eyed stares from the unsuspecting tourists nearby. Maddux didn't wait around to watch the water plummet back down into Lake Alpsee. He snatched his bag off the ground and turned toward the mountainside.

In the distance, he spotted Ingrid running into the woods.

XXX

INGRID VANISHED INTO THE THICK pine trees rising above the lake. Venturing after her in the woods wasn't a task Maddux relished, yet he couldn't let her go. There was Astrid to think of—and Voss.

As Maddux hustled toward the last place he saw Ingrid, he wondered about her comments regarding Voss.

Was Voss really a double spy? Had he been playing the U.S. this whole time? Did he really know about Ingrid's KGB training?

Maddux struggled to believe it, though Barbara had warned him that naiveté would get him killed one day. "Trust no one," she'd told him, yet such an axiom failed in principle despite seeming wise. Maddux had believed Voss. But now the young spy wondered if that trust cobbled around a façade of lies. He concluded that perhaps he only assumed everything was true out of a desperate attempt to reconnect with his father.

But the truth about his father—and everything else—was still out there. Finding Ingrid might give him one more crack at separating fact from fiction as it pertained to his father and the other mysteries haunting his mind.

Maddux put aside the tormenting thought as he entered the forest, instead focusing on tracking down Ingrid. As he moved deeper into the trees, he asked himself what he would do if he wanted to escape someone.

The caves.

Near the top of the ledge, a thick swath of trees shrouded a series of caverns. Maddux had read about them in a travel magazine while he was preparing for the operation. Such a locale would be the perfect place to hide, if not ambush those pursuing you.

After ten minutes of hiking up the hill, Maddux cautiously neared the caves. He remained 200 meters away before sliding down behind a rock and assembling his rifle. The trees groaned as a large gust of wind whipped across the mountain, the smell of fresh pine wafting along the breeze.

Maddux inserted a bullet into the chamber and brushed off the scope. Lying prone, he positioned himself between a pair of rocks that had a narrow opening between them so that he would be barely visible—if at all—to anyone in the caves.

Now all Maddux could do was wait.

He reviewed all of his sniper training during his time preparing with the CIA. Despite Pritchett's insistence that this mission wouldn't be as complicated as it sounded, Maddux never imagined himself needing to shoot a KGB operative from long distance to consider this a success.

The minutes dripped past like hours until Maddux noticed some movement in the shadows. He slowed his breathing as a silhouetted figure ventured out from the cave. When the person turned around, Maddux recognized Ingrid immediately. Without wasting any time, he sited her in and prepared to pull the trigger. He slowly exhaled and squeezed.

Crack!

The shot echoed through the woods, only a fraction of a second before a bullet ripped through Ingrid. She stumbled to the ground and lay motionless.

Maddux grabbed his pack and raced up the hill toward her. When he arrived, she was lying prone on the ground, moaning softly from the pain. He kept his gun trained on her, his finger on the trigger.

"If you shoot me, you'll never know where my daughter is," Ingrid said. "I know Otto would want to see her again."

Maddux shook his head. "Do you think that's going to work with me?"

"You can believe whatever you want to believe. Your masters at the CIA are good at manipulating impressionable minds."

"You think I'm CIA. Now, that's some good KGB fiction."

"Don't try to fool me. I know all the signs, even if I don't know who you are."

Maddux slid to the side, trying to get a better position to shoot her in case she made a quick movement. "Otto never told you about me?"

"No, the only way I could ever get information off him was to bug him. He was a lousy husband when it came to conversation, especially pillow talk."

"Well, he told me all about you. And he seemed pretty upset about the revelation that you were KGB."

"He's a good liar."

"No," Maddux said, kicking at the dirt. "You can end your little story right there. I'm not buying it. He's not that good of an actor."

"Believe what you will. But just know that I don't want to kill you," she said. "If you'll let me go, I'll tell you where my daughter is. You wouldn't want her to die, now would you?"

"And you would?" Maddux asked. "What kind of mother are you?"

"The kind of mother who would do whatever she needed to do for her country. While I have grown fond of Astrid, she was all part of my cover."

"But not Otto's?"

Ingrid rolled onto her side, hands raised in the air in a posture of surrender. "Can we stop this charade? Please put your weapon down and I will tell you about my daughter. Then you can let me go. How does that sound?"

"I'm not sure my superiors would appreciate such a move."

"I can tell you're a new spy, Mr.—"

"Jackson," Maddux said. "Theodore Jackson."

"Well, *Teddy*, if there's one good giveaway for a new spy, it's that he thinks he can convince someone else that there is someone to answer to. A seasoned spy doesn't make such a rookie mistake. You just do whatever you need to do in order to survive and complete the mission."

"My mission has already been completed," Maddux said. "I snuffed out your plan to bomb the lab."

"So you did," she said. "But you decided to risk your

own life to come after me. Why?"

"For Otto and Astrid."

"Hmm. A noble spy—how novel."

"Nobility has nothing to do with my decision to come after you, but it had everything to do with an opportunity to capture you."

"You're very confident in your skills. It will be your downfall."

In a flash, Ingrid reached behind her neck and pulled a gun out of her shirt. She rolled to her left and fired a shot at Maddux, hitting him in his left arm. He dropped his gun and fell to the ground.

Ingrid staggered to her feet, dragging her right leg behind her where Maddux's earlier bullet had hit.

"Where's Astrid?" Maddux asked, grimacing from the pain.

"What does it matter?" she asked. "You're about to die. But if that's what you want to know before I put a bullet in you, she's staying at the Neuschwanstein Inn just down the road in Room 43."

"Thanks," Maddux said.

He reached for the gun in his pocket and Ingrid kicked him in the face, knocking his weapon aside.

"You have plenty of—how do you Americans say it?—*moxie*? Too bad it will be for naught."

A gunshot reverberated through the woods, sending birds flying and squirrels scampering nearby.

XXXI

MADDUX STARED AT HIS ARM where blood gushed out at an alarming rate. His face still throbbed from the vicious kick Ingrid had delivered just moments earlier, effectively ending his chances of winning the standoff with the KGB operative. She'd gained the upper hand by relying on veteran tactics. However, she made one rookie mistake: she thought Maddux was alone.

Maddux staggered to his feet and stepped over Ingrid. Her eyes widened as she gasped for air.

"My partner stuck around longer than yours did," Maddux said. "I'll be sure to let Astrid know how much you loved her."

Ingrid flailed at him, struggling to say something.

Maddux stopped and crouched near to hear what she was saying. "What was that?"

"What do you want me to tell your father?" she asked, barely louder than a whisper.

Maddux shook his head. "Even if he weren't dead, I doubt you'd be seeing him."

Ingrid tried to say something again before she took

one final breath and then died. Maddux stared at her lifeless body for a moment before scanning the ridge and spotting Barbara. She raised her rifle triumphantly before heading toward Maddux.

Grabbing Ingrid's gun off the ground, Maddux stuffed the weapon in his belt. He then removed Ingrid's locket. He opened it and peered inside at the picture, one of Ingrid with her daughter.

"Liar," Maddux muttered before collapsing at the foot of a tree. He awoke a few minutes later to Barbara's voice as his partner hovered over him.

"You still with us?" Barbara asked.

Maddux opened his eyes and nodded. He grabbed his arm, which Barbara immediately began to tend to.

"Good work out there today," Barbara said as she dressed his wounds.

"I couldn't have done it without you," Maddux said. "You'd be making funeral plans instead of fixing me up if you hadn't been here, too."

"Don't be so modest," she said. "You're the one who removed the bomb and saved everyone."

"What happened with the lab?" he asked as he sat up.

"They did their homework and sabotaged the entrance. We couldn't get anyone out in time."

"I figured as much when I didn't see your signal."

"But even after you stopped the bomb, you still went after Ingrid."

Maddux shrugged. "She knew too much. After all, she was the real spy."

"Nevertheless, that showed some guts."

"And fortunately you were there for me. Nice shooting, by the way."

Barbara smiled and stroked his face with the back of her hand. "We're a good team, Maddux."

"Yeah, we are. Now, let's not do anything to ruin it, okay?"

Barbara withdrew and nodded, signaling that she understood what he implied.

* * *

TWO DAYS LATER, Maddux and Barbara eased into their chairs across from Pritchett in his office. He clasped his hands and leaned forward, the corners of his mouth edging slightly upward.

"Excellent work out there, both of you," Pritchett said, his left eye darting back and forth between the two agents.

Then he focused his attention on Maddux. "You mind telling me why you continued to pursue Ingrid?"

"Instinct, I guess," Maddux said. "I just knew I couldn't let her get away. I also had a feeling about her."

"Well, trust you gut more often in the future, Maddux," Pritchett said. "Turns out that Ingrid was far more than just a KGB operative. She was one of their top assassins. We were even able to find evidence that she had been staking out one of our leading scientists."

"She was quite the Trojan horse," Barbara said.

"More than you know," Pritchett said. "We also found these on her after you two took care of her." He pushed across a small plastic bag that contained several microdots.

"What was on them?" Maddux asked.

"Information about our research, key scientists with their addresses and family members, details on some of our operatives—the intelligence that she amassed in such a short period of time was jaw-dropping."

"What happened to the body?" Barbara asked.

"We incinerated it," Pritchett said. "There's no telling where else she may have hidden intel. We weren't about to take a chance and notify the Russians. But they won't be asking any questions about her, that much we're sure of. They know better than that."

"And what about Dr. Voss?" Maddux asked.

"What about him?" Pritchett said.

"Are we sure he's on our side?"

Pritchett shrugged. "There's no way to be sure, but if I had to stake my life on one side or the other, I'd say he was on our side. As in all situations, be careful what you say to him."

"So what's next?"

Pritchett opened his top desk drawer and pulled out Ingrid's locket. "There's someone in the lobby who'd love to speak to you."

"Why don't you do it, Barbara?" Maddux asked. "You'd probably be better at comforting a little girl than I would."

Barbara shook her head. "She's going to want to hear from you, not me. You were the one that was with her when she died. Tell Astrid something about her mother that won't make her hate her."

"I'm not sure I can do that," Maddux said.

"You'll think of something."

They both stood and exited Pritchett's office.

"Good luck," Barbara said as they walked down the hallway.

She peeled off to the left, leaving Maddux to walk

down the corridor to the elevator lobby. He wasn't excited about engaging Astrid in a conversation about her mother, but someone had to do it. And Barbara was probably correct in assigning him the task. He was the one who had the most interaction with Ingrid and was standing right by her side when she died.

When Maddux reached the elevator, he pressed the down button and waited. He clutched the locket in his hand and contemplated what to say as he stepped inside. His contemplative moment was interrupted by another agent.

"First time with a surviving dependent?" a man asked.

Maddux looked up to lock eyes with another operative before nodding.

"It's never easy," he said. "But be honest. The truth does far more to heal the wounds than a lie."

"Thanks," Maddux said as he opened his hand and stared at the locket.

When the elevator reached the ground floor, a bell dinged and the doors slid open. He stepped into the lobby and spotted Voss with his young daughter.

"How are you two doing?" Maddux asked as he walked over toward them.

"Under the circumstances, I think we're fine," Voss said. "I can't thank you enough for getting me back Astrid."

Astrid smiled briefly and threw her right arm around her father. Maddux could tell she was doing everything she could not to cry.

He stooped low and held out his hands in front of Astrid. "I brought you something."

"What's this?" she asked.

"It was your mother's," Maddux said. "She would've wanted you to have this."

"Did you talk to her, you know, before she died?"

Maddux nodded. "She wanted me to tell you how much she loved you, even though she was sure you wouldn't understand why she did what she did."

"Was my mother good?" Astrid asked.

Maddux took a deep breath and stared off in the distance before answering her. "Your mother loved you—and that's what's important."

Maddux glanced up at Voss, who nodded and mouthed a *thank you.*

"Will I be seeing you again?" Maddux asked Voss.

Voss shrugged. "I don't know, but I know we're leaving Germany. We need a fresh start—both of us."

"I understand," Maddux said. "Good luck to both of you."

Voss shook Maddux's hand and then put his arm around Astrid before ushering her out of the building.

Maddux watched them leave, lingering for a moment. He wondered if he'd said the right thing, even though he'd twisted the truth.

He snapped back to reality when he felt a file hit his chest. Maddux looked down and put his hands on the folder before looking up at Pritchett.

"I promised you something," Pritchett said, "and I want you to know that I'm a man of my word."

"What is this?" Maddux asked.

"It's a dossier on your father. I wish it was more comprehensive, but it's all I've got. It's *everything* we've got."

Maddux thanked Pritchett and glanced down at the folder. Maddux's hands shook as he opened it and started reading. The first name he saw jumped off the page at him: John Hambrick. It didn't take long before Maddux's eyes bulged wide as he took in the new information about his father's past.

Maddux looked up to see Pritchett still standing there.

"I have some more questions for you about this," Maddux said.

Pritchett nodded knowingly. "I thought you might."

XXXII

MADDUX GAWKED AS HE SCANNED the overhead beams supporting the ceiling of the Em Höttche restaurant a block away from the banks of the Rhine River. History oozed from the walls as craftsmanship from a bygone era decorated every nook and cranny. Though there was a plaque in the lobby detailing the restaurant's fabled past, Maddux thought the history lesson wasn't necessary given the musky wood odor and the interior design.

"So did Beethoven really used to dine here?" Rose Fuller asked as she sat down across from Maddux.

"That's what the sign says," Maddux said with a shrug. "Whether it's true or not, this place has obviously seen its fair share of history through the years."

"I hope the food is as good as stories."

A waiter appeared and took their drink orders before disappearing into the kitchen.

"I'm glad you made it back," Rose said. "I heard the mission was a little dicey."

"That's one way of putting it. But I'm sure it would've been far more challenging without all your gadgets."

"I was wondering how the tie clip worked out," she said.

"It came in handy, but not as much as the watch did. That thing saved my life."

"That's good to hear. I find all feedback from field agents to be helpful in constructing future tech."

The waiter returned with their glasses of wine before taking their dinner order and promptly leaving.

"Did Pritchett keep his word?" Rose asked.

Maddux nodded. "Pritchett finally got approval to give me the file on my father. It was quite eye-opening."

"Want to talk about it?"

"It might do me some good," Maddux said before taking a long pull on his wine glass.

Rose held up her glass and clinked it with Maddux's. "Cheers," she said. "Now, I'm all ears."

"The KGB first approached my father about going to work for them," Maddux began. "Of course, he was reluctant to engage in any such offer, but he'd begun climbing the ladder within the scientific community and was becoming well known. Apparently, the KGB saw an opportunity to steal one of the bright young minds— even in his early forties—away from the U.S. stable of scientists. My father grew increasingly uncomfortable with the pressure the KGB was exerting on him, and he decided to meet with the CIA. He met with the New York station chief, who urged my father to sign up as a civilian agent and relent before the KGB's persuasive tactics reverted to a stronger form of coercion."

"So, the CIA thought the KGB might force your father to work for them?" Rose asked.

"Yes—and if he didn't, the CIA thought the KGB might kill him."

"Are you sure this wasn't the CIA's way of recruiting a spy that could easily infiltrate the KGB's scientific research circle?"

"That was my first thought, too. And I'm still not sure if I've landed on any conclusion. The agency is opportunistic, that's for sure. But this still could've been genuine. I haven't read much about the KGB's coercive tactics yet."

"From what I understand, the KGB is relentless."

Maddux drank more of his wine and nodded.

"They are, which is why I tend to lean toward the CIA telling my father the truth in this situation."

"So, your father took them up on it apparently, right?"

"He convinced the KGB that the best way to move forward was for everyone to think he was dead. Honestly, the move was a stroke of genius as it pertains to espionage. His peers wouldn't search for him because everyone would assume he was gone."

"So, he took on a new identity?"

"Dr. John Hambrick. The KGB even falsified his credentials so he could attend conferences in Europe and other places around the world. He worked in Prague as well as Moscow, developing weapons systems for the KGB."

"And he kept the CIA informed of everything?"

"Up until about three years ago."

"What happened then?"

"My father vanished. Nobody knows what happened to him. They would've taken the opportunity to castigate the U.S. if he'd been caught spying. But there wasn't a peep about his disappearance. No whispers from our listening channels about what could've happened to him. Nothing. Zilch."

"And the U.S. hasn't heard from him either, I assume."

"That's right. He has protocols for contacting the CIA and my mother."

"Your mother knew about this?"

Maddux sighed. "I haven't spoken with her about this, but I found a letter from my father in her drawer. Apparently, they've been communicating for a while."

"You didn't ask her about this?"

"I try to avoid uncomfortable conversations with my mother," he said. "I'm not afraid of confrontation, but I was too upset to ask her about it at the time."

"And since then?"

"I could have, I guess. But I wanted to know the CIA's side of the story, official or not, before I said anything. Now that I know, I'm still not sure I want to broach the subject with her."

"So, wait a minute. If your father has truly disappeared, what about those photos Alexi showed you in New York?"

"That was one of the questions I had for Pritchett after I read this. He told me that they were faked and that the CIA does that all the time. Some good ole spy magic."

"Science," Rose corrected him. "There's no such thing as magic."

"I'm still not sure I believe it because it looked like he was holding a newspaper from that day."

Rose smiled. "I know how to do this—and it's not as difficult as you might think. But it still takes some technical skill, scientifically speaking, of course."

Maddux laughed softly. "Of course."

"So, what's your gut telling you?"

"I just don't know. I haven't spoken to my mother about the letter yet, but it looked like it was routed through the CIA somehow before it got to her."

"Maybe you should talk to her then and find out if she's heard from him through some other method."

"That will be an awkward conversation, though one I need to have in person instead of over the phone."

"I agree. When are you going back home again?"

Maddux exhaled slowly and looked around the restaurant. "As weird as it might sound to hear this, Germany is home now. I know I need to visit my mother at some point, but I think I'm going to be here for a long time."

"If there's one thing I've learned in my time with the agency, it's that you should never get comfortable or make any assumptions about anything. You might be working in India next month if they need you there."

"If you're still here, let's hope not," Maddux said with a wink.

* * *

MADDUX PARTED WAYS with Rose at the bus stop after dinner. He would've preferred to do the gentlemanly thing and walk her home, but Maddux was already tempting fate by going out to dinner with her. If the KGB learned that he was CIA and put him under surveillance, all of Maddux's relationships at the agency were endangered by public meetings. And ultimately, Rose's safety was more important than keeping up some image he'd concocted of himself: a gentleman and a spy. He concluded he could be both at the same time, though perhaps one would have to surrender to the other on occasion. And this was one of those times.

He walked home and reflected on his conversation with Rose, thinking mostly about what he said regarding his father. Could something tragic have happened to him? Or was there a new angle to play, a new world of secrets to uncover? Maddux wasn't sure and didn't have a feeling one way or another.

If only I could speak with him . . . .

Several minutes later, he sauntered up the steps to his home and unlocked the front door. As he flung it open, he stepped inside and heard something crackle beneath his feet. Sliding to the side, he shut the door before stooping down to pick up a large manila folder along with a small white envelope.

Recognizing the Prague station's secret address, Maddux ripped open the package and pulled out a copy of the *Lidové noviny* from September 12, 1952.

Well, what do ya know? Norton delivered.

Maddux rifled through the pages, unsure of what he was looking for before the handwriting on the envelope caught his eye. He set the paper down and tore open the letter.

Dear Son,

I wanted to write you and tell you not to worry about me. I've missed you terribly over the years, but I did what I had to do. I can't tell you what's happening or why I went silent toward the agency, but just know that one day I'll tell you everything.

In the meantime, know that I'm very proud

of you and all that you've done to protect your country and fellow countrymen. Your actions serve as a reminder that I made the right decision many years ago even though it went against almost everything I'd ever believed.

Keep making me proud, Son. You are a good man . . . the best.

Love,
Dad

Maddux placed his back against the wall and slid to the floor, emotions overrunning him. He prided himself on rarely crying, but he couldn't stop the flow of tears after reading his father's emotional missive.

After a few minutes, Maddux wiped away the tears and stood. He felt more resolve than ever to track down his father.

THE END

ACKNOWLEDGMENTS

Starting a new series is always frightening territory for an author. Until readers start tearing into a story, I always wonder if they are going to resonate with my characters and with the storyline. So far, the feedback I've received on the first book in the Ed Maddux series has been encouraging, and I hope that continues as the series progresses.

The bulk of my research for this novel took place at the National Archives, and I'm incredibly grateful to Steven Hamilton for his direction there. Finding these CIA papers from the 1960s wasn't easy, and I doubt I would've ever thought to look for them had it not been for him.

I'm also grateful for the assistance provided by Boston University professor, Dr. Igor Lukes. His book, *On the Edge of the Cold War*, is one I'd highly recommend for further nonfiction reading on espionage during this time period in Czechoslovakia. He also was kind enough to take the time to answer specific questions I had regarding small details surrounding espionage and border patrol during the 1960s, which found their way into this book.

As usual, I appreciate the editing skills of Krystal Wade and Brooke Turbyfill in making sure this book isn't riddled with mistakes.

And as always, I must thank my wife for listening to me babble on about espionage while I worked away on crafting this story.

Last but not least, I want to thank you, the reader, for supporting my work. I hope you enjoyed reading this book as much as I enjoyed writing it.

NEWSLETTER SIGNUP

If you would like to stay up to date on R.J. Patterson's latest writing projects with his periodic newsletter, sign up at www.RJPbooks.com.

ABOUT THE AUTHOR

R.J. PATTERSON is an award-winning writer living in the Pacific Northwest. He first began his illustrious writing career as a sports journalist, recording his exploits on the soccer fields in England as a young boy. Then when his father told him that people would pay him to watch sports if he would write about what he saw, he went all in. He landed his first writing job at age 15 as a sports writer for a daily newspaper in Orangeburg, S.C. He later attended earned a degree in newspaper journalism from the University of Georgia, where he took a job covering high school sports for the award-winning *Athens Banner-Herald* and *Daily News*.

He later became the sports editor of *The Valdosta Daily Times* before working in the magazine world as an editor and freelance journalist. He has won numerous writing awards, including a national award for his investigative reporting on a sordid tale surrounding an NCAA investigation over the University of Georgia football program.

R.J. enjoys the great outdoors of the Northwest while living there with his wife and four children. He still follows sports closely and enjoys coaching his daughter's soccer team.

He also loves connecting with readers and would love to hear from you. To stay updated about future projects, connect with him over Facebook, on Twitter or Instagram (@MrRJPatterson) or on the interwebs at:

www.RJPbooks.com